God's Gift

A STORY OF FAITH, FAMILY, AND FOOTBALL

Todd Mills

ISBN 978-1-0980-8128-7 (paperback)
ISBN 978-1-0980-8191-1 (hardcover)
ISBN 978-1-0980-8129-4 (digital)

Christian Faith Publishing, Inc.
832 Park Avenue
Meadville, PA 16335
www.christianfaithpublishing.com

Printed in the United States of America

To my three angels in heaven. I love you.

For by grace you have been saved through faith. And this is not your own doing, it is the gift of God, not a result of works, so that no one may boast.

—Ephesians 2:8–9 (ESV)

CONTENTS

CHAPTER 1

— ∾ —

Rise and Shine

It was eight forty-five on a warm and sunny Sunday morning in September. Seventeen-year-old Jimmy Lawson was buried under the pillows and blankets of his bed in a deep sleep. As the fan near his bed blew cool air throughout the room, the sun rose and beams of light pierced through the blinds of his windows. Suddenly the door opened abruptly.

"Jim," his mom, Deborah, said in a soft voice as she approached the side of his bed. She then sat down lightly near the head of the bed, placed her hand gently on Jimmy's back, and said, "Jimmy, wake up, honey, it's time for church."

As Jimmy groaned and slightly squirmed, she pulled the blanket from over his head and said in a sweet but stern tone, "Get up, honey, it's almost nine, and you're not gonna make us late again this week.

You have thirty minutes to get up, take a shower, and get dressed."

She then got up from the bed, but before she left the room, she walked over to the window and opened the blinds. Which let more light in and made it harder for Jimmy to continue sleeping. As she left the room, Jimmy rolled out of his blankets and sat on the side of his bed, with his elbows on his knees and his face in his hands. He then let out a sharp exhale, got up, and went into the bathroom to take a shower.

See, Jimmy and his parents had been going to church together every Sunday morning for as long as he could remember. But after Jimmy's dad, who was a police detective, was killed during an undercover investigation, it had just been him and his mom. Although Jimmy grew up going to church every week, it didn't make getting up and sitting through the two-hour Sunday service any easier. Although he didn't mind hearing a positive message, he'd rather be sleeping in until the NFL games came on TV, like most of his friends were doing. Jimmy believed in the teachings of the Bible, but as a seventeen-year-old high school football player, that was being recruited by many of the major Division 1 college football programs in the country, he's more focused on scoring touchdowns, getting interceptions, and choosing a date for Vickroy High School's upcoming homecoming dance.

As he got dressed, he got a text from his best friend, Sean, Vickroy High School's starting quarterback.

> I saw miss Jennings at the grocery store last night and she asked me who ur planning to take to the dance.
>
> She's praying u take Emily lol

Jimmy read the text and smiled but didn't reply. His charming smile and charismatic personality had won the hearts of not only every girl in school but of everyone in town who knew him. Ms. Jennings was his algebra teacher, and she thought the world of Jimmy. Not because he was a high school football star but because she thought he was the smartest kid in school, had a great personality, and had a Christian upbringing. Nothing would have made her happier than seeing her daughter, Emily, go to the homecoming dance with Jimmy, whom she had a crush on since elementary school.

As Jimmy tied his shoes, his phone vibrated again, but just before he pulled it out of his pocket, his mom peeked her head in the door, tossed him her car keys, and said, "I'm ready, let's go."

Jimmy only had his learner's permit, but he always drove his mom to church on Sunday mornings because she liked to close her eyes and sing along to the gospel songs on the radio on the way in.

When they arrived at church, Jimmy and his mom took their seats in the balcony together where they always sat. As the choir began to sing, his mom stood to sing along, and Jimmy drifted off into a daydream about Friday night's impressive 28–0 win against Merryville High School who went 8–2 last year and boasted one of the best defenses in the district. Everyone expected Jimmy to have a breakout season, but 110 rushing yards on just six carries, five receptions for 105 yards, three touchdowns, and an interception on defense in the season opener was a performance that had the entire state of Pennsylvania buzzing. The previous year, as a sophomore, Jimmy set conference records for all-purpose yards and total touchdowns in a season and was an all-state selection, but after an offseason in which he hit the weights like never before, put on fifteen pounds of muscle and grew two inches, the 6'1" 195-pound junior had plans to win a state championship and get a scholarship official offer from his favorite college football team, the University of Alabama Crimson Tide.

As the choir finished their songs and the preacher began to take the stage, Jimmy snapped out of his daydream and focused his attention at the pulpit in preparation to hear the message.

The preacher opened his Bible and said, "Today I'm going to preach out of the book of Romans, so if you have your Bibles, tablets, smartphones, go with me to Romans chapter 3." While the preacher gave everyone time to turn to the scripture, Jimmy received a text message from Samantha, a girl at school that he had been hanging out with lately.

GOD'S GIFT

> Hey you! 😊 Good game on Friday! You guys gonna win states this year??

> Haha, thanks. U kno it!

> Please beat Central Catholic. I'm sick of hearing them brag about beating us in the first round last year

> Yeah this year will be different
>
> Delivered

> Good. What r u guys doin after the game on Friday?

> I'm not sure. I'm sure everyone is gonna wanna go celebrate after we win

> 😊 u guys better win. None of u ever go out after u lose and I wanna see u this weekend...

> Haha, I got u. I'll make sure we take care of business on the field. Just let me know what u end up doing after the game and I'll swing thru
>
> Delivered

While Jimmy had this conversation with Samantha, the preacher began teaching his message out of the book of Romans. "Let's start at verse 20. The word of God reads:

For no one can ever be made right with God by doing what the law commands. The law simply shows us how sinful we are. But now God has shown us a way to be made right with him without keeping the requirements of the law, as was promised in the writings of Moses and the prophets long ago. We are made right with God by placing our faith in Jesus Christ. And this is true for everyone who believes, no matter who we are. For everyone has sinned; we all fall short of God's glorious standard. Yet God, in his grace, freely makes us right in his sight. He did this through Christ Jesus when he freed us from the penalty for our sins. For God presented Jesus as the sacrifice for sin. People are made right with God when they believe that Jesus sacrificed his life, shedding his blood. This sacrifice shows that God was being fair when he held back and did not punish those who sinned in times past, for he was looking ahead and including them in what he would do in this present time. God did this to demonstrate his righteousness, for He himself is fair and just, and he makes sinners right in his sight when they believe in Jesus. Can we boast, then, that we have done anything to be accepted by God? No, because our acquittal is not based on obeying the law. It is based on faith. So we are made right with God through faith and not by obeying the law.

"These verses are from a letter that the Apostle Paul wrote to the Romans about the good news of our Lord Jesus Christ. In this chapter, Paul is explaining to the Roman people that we are all sinners, Jews and Gentiles, those of us that are law-abiding citizens, and those of us that are criminals, those that claim to follow Christ, and those that are atheist, so we cannot earn our salvation through good deeds and by following the law. But the good news is that God showed us His amazing grace by giving us the gift of His Son, which allows us all to have salvation that we don't deserve. All we have to do is believe and place our hope and our faith in Him. Therefore, no one can take any credit for their salvation. No one can say that they were saved because they worked hard or made sacrifices. But instead, we all will have to fall to our knees and give all praise to God for His grace. So I encourage you, brothers and sisters, place all your hopes, all your dreams, and all of your faith in Christ. For we know that our lives on this side and the other are better off in His hands than in our own."

As the pastor concluded his message, Jimmy got up and went to the car to pull it to the front for his mom. As he left, Deborah bowed her head and began to pray for him. She was so proud of the young man that he was with all of his talents and all that he had accomplished, but she worried about the temptations that came along with success in sports. She wanted him to understand the importance of keeping God first through the highs in life because she knew how devastating the lows would be if he didn't have his faith as his foundation.

Once the service was dismissed, Jimmy and his mom went back home to eat Sunday dinner together which was another weekly tradition at the Lawsons. Deborah didn't like the TV on while they ate because Jimmy would just be distracted by the NFL football games, so instead, Jimmy ate his dinner while reading the local news sports section on his tablet. Deborah was obviously troubled by something, but Jimmy didn't notice because he was so interested in the article that he was reading. Once he finished eating, he got up to take his plate to the kitchen, but before he left the table, Deborah stopped him.

"Jim," she said in a concerned tone. "I know you're sick of hearing it, but you're turning eighteen in a few months, and the next few years will be critical in determining what type of man you will be for the rest of your life. I want you to really start taking your faith seriously. God has blessed you with so much talent, you're smart, charming, handsome—"

Jimmy suddenly cut her off, smiled, and said in a reassuring tone, "And Pennsylvania's next athlete of the year," as he handed her the tablet he was reading.

Deborah looked at the tablet and saw the headline of the article that Jimmy was reading which read "God's Gift to Football Fans" over a big picture of Jimmy running the football in last Friday's game.

She scoffed and continued in a soft tone, "Just don't take it all for granted, son. Remember, you are blessed to be a blessing to others, and God deserves all of the credit for everything you have."

Jimmy looked her in the eyes sincerely and said, "I hear you, Ma, I love you, okay?" Then he gave her an endearing kiss before he walked out of the room to go watch football.

The following morning was much different than Sunday morning when Jimmy's mom had to come in to wake him for church. On Monday, Jimmy woke up at 5:00 a.m. without setting an alarm. He was up early because he wanted to get to school before 6:00 a.m. to work out in the gym for an hour before class started at 7:15 a.m.

This type of commitment and dedication was unusual for the average seventeen-year-old kid, but he was driven. Football was his passion, and he worked his butt off to be the best, and that was what was different about Jimmy. He wasn't just talented, he was the hardest worker on his team, and he played with a fire in his eyes that his coaches said they had never seen before. Maybe he worked so hard because he wasn't always the best. Growing up, people used to tell him that he was too small to play high school football and that he would get hurt. But they aren't saying things like that anymore. Jimmy used that doubt to fuel him to outwork everyone and become one of the best high school players in the country, but he wasn't satisfied. He trained with his eyes set on playing at a Division 1 college and then the NFL.

When Jimmy got out of bed, he first went downstairs to the kitchen to boil eggs for his breakfast. While the eggs were boiling, he got dressed, brushed his teeth, and got his book bag packed for school. He then packed a separate duffel bag for his workout and practice gear. Once his bags were all packed, he went back into the kitchen, put his hardboiled eggs in a sandwich bag, and threw them in his duffel bag. Then he threw his bags over his shoulders and walked out the door. Jimmy and his mom only lived about a mile from the school, so he walked to the school every morning except on game days. As he walked, it was still dark, no cars were out on the road yet, and the birds were still asleep. The air was cool, and the quiet breeze was all that made a sound. This peaceful commute served as the perfect calm before the storm that took place in the gym every morning Monday through Thursday.

When he got to the school, he walked around to the back entrance of the gym and used the key Coach Thomas, his head coach, gave him to get in. He went in the weight room, turned on the lights, and walked straight over to the auxiliary cord where he plugged in his phone to play his playlist through the sound system speakers. Jimmy's playlist was a compilation of his favorite hip-hop tracks. As the music began to play, he started bobbing his head, walked over to his duffel bag, and pulled out his elevation mask that he wore during his workouts to improve his stamina and endurance. He also liked wearing it because it made him look like Bane from Batman and made him feel like a beast in the gym. He strapped his mask on, grabbed two twenty-five-pound weight plates, and got on the treadmill.

As the music blared through the speakers, he started his workout running a mile on the treadmill while carrying the 25-pound weights in his hands. He then went to the squat rack and squatted 315 pounds for five sets of ten. After squats he went into box jumps and single-leg plyometrics. He trained with focus, his pace was steady, and there were very little breaks in between his sets. When he got done with plyometrics, he grabbed a set of 25-pound dumbbells and did a shoulder circuit consisting of presses, front raises, and lateral raises. To complete his workout, Jimmy went to his bag and pulled out his jump rope and did one hundred single-leg double-unders.

As he was finishing his last set of double-unders, his buddy, Sean, was walking in. As Sean walked down the hall, approaching the weight room, he could hear the sound of Jimmy's jump rope whipping through the air and tapping the gym floor, along with the sound of his deep respirations coming through the elevation mask. When he walked in, he saw Jimmy jumping rope in a puddle of sweat with his back to the door, still looking up at the clock on the wall.

"Deuce!" Sean said to get Jimmy's attention. Most of Jimmy's teammates and coaches called him that in reference to his football jersey number. Jimmy stopped, turned around, took off his mask, and smiled.

"What's up, bro?" Jimmy said, breathing heavily.

"What's up? You done?"

"Yeah, gotta hop in the shower real quick before everyone else starts rollin' in."

"You better make it quick, it's six forty-five."

"I know, I know," Jimmy replied as he threw his things in his bag and jogged out of the weight room and into the locker room.

"I'll wait for you in here," Sean yelled as the locker room door was closing.

Once Jimmy got dressed, in his usual athletic look wearing sweatpants and a T-shirt, he and Sean started heading to class while he drank his post-workout shake.

As they walked through the halls, most of the underclassmen stepped to the side to make way as they looked at Jimmy and Sean in admiration, all of the girls blushed and giggled as they said hi, and most of the teachers stopped to congratulate them on last Friday's win. The school spirit at Vickroy was at an all-time high, and there was an excitement in the atmosphere that was just infectious. The cheerleaders had the entire school decorated and decked out with black-and-gold banners and streamers everywhere. The realistic possibility of a state championship was something that everyone that had any connection to the school was excited to be a part of.

"Hey, guys," Emily said as she came from behind.

"Oh, what's up, Em?" Jimmy said as he put his arm around her, while they continued walking down the hall.

"Yo, Em, I saw your mom at the grocery store on Saturday," Sean said.

"Yeah, she told me. She said you were trying to get out of turning in your algebra homework too."

"Well, I had a lot going on this weekend," Sean said, laughing.

"Yeah, sure. I'll see you guys later," Emily said, giggling as she gave Jimmy a hug and walked in her classroom.

"Yo, Lawson, three touchdowns and you basically only played the first half!" one of their classmates said as he approached.

"Thanks, man, we're on a mission," Jimmy said, smiling as they stopped and exchanged handshakes.

"I can't wait for the Central game!" the classmate said.

"Patience, my brother, we gotta take it one game at a time. We're only focused on East Liberty right now," Jimmy said.

"We won't be seeing Central until the playoffs anyway, so slow your roll," Sean said.

"I know, but I can't stand them, and I know you guys will beat them this year with the way you two played on Friday," the classmate said.

Jimmy and Sean looked at each other and smiled as Sean shrugged his shoulders and said, chuckling, "Well, he is right."

Sean was also being recruited by Division 1 colleges and had a breakout game of his own on Friday. He completed all fifteen of his pass attempts for 140 yards and a touchdown. He also had 43 yards rushing. He was looking to improve on his standout sophomore season as well, which earned him third team all-state honors. At 5'11", 170 pounds, he was a little undersized to be a Division 1 quarterback but was still one of the best athletes in the state, and with this duo leading the way, Vickroy High was likely to be contending for the state title.

As they continued down the hall, Sean nudged Jimmy with his elbow. "Here comes Samantha."

"Hi, God's gift to football," she said while smiling at Jimmy.

"What's up? You saw that article, huh?" Jimmy laughed.

"Yes, I did, and I was hoping I would see you this morning because I'm having a party at my house after the game on Friday, and I wanted you two to be the first to know."

"Sweet. We'll be there," Sean quickly replied.

"You better. And tell your teammates and whoever else you want to invite."

"Okay, cool. Thanks for the invitation," Jimmy said.

"Of course," Samantha said as she smiled and gave Jimmy a hug.

Once she walked away, Sean laughed and said, "I think that was an invitation to something a little more than a party."

"Whatever, man," Jimmy replied as he laughed and gave Sean a pound before he went in the classroom.

"Yeah, you know it was. I'll see you at lunch."

"All right, later," Jimmy said as the teacher closed the classroom door.

Later on, after a slow-paced practice, which mainly consisted of offensive play installation, a handful of guys from the team met up at the G Bar. The G Bar was a local pub in town that the guys liked to go to for 25-cents wing night, which had become a weekly tradition during the season. When Jimmy and Sean got there, offensive lineman Brandon Rice and linebacker Jeremy Rowley were already there getting started.

"How did I know y'all would be in here already eating?" Sean said, smiling and shaking his head.

"We came straight from practice, bro," Brandon replied while licking wing sauce from his fingers.

"Who's all coming?" Jimmy asked.

"EJ, Tim, and Days all said they're on the way," Jeremy said.

"Cool, well, no need to waste time. I'm gonna get started," Jimmy replied.

"Me too," Sean said as he gestured to get the waitress's attention. Jimmy and Sean placed their wing orders as the rest of the guys walked in the door.

"*Hey*, nice of you guys to finally show up," Jimmy joked.

"Tim took forever, talking about he had to finish writing a paper, and this fool still gets in my car with a textbook in his hand," EJ said.

"Man, I got a physics test tomorrow, so I gotta study tonight. It was either bring my books or miss wing night," said Tim.

"Don't mind these guys, man, do what you gotta do. We all know you're gonna ace that test tomorrow anyway, Ivy League," Jimmy said, laughing.

"Don't speak too soon. Gotta make sure I maintain my 4.0 GPA this year, or I could lose my scholarship. That's why I really gotta buckle down. Don't wanna blow it," Tim Hall said, laughing.

"Right, stop giving him a hard time, EJ," Brandon Rice said.

"All right, all right, my bad, bro," said EJ.

Brandon didn't talk much, but when he did, people listened. At 6'5" and 280 pounds, his presence alone commanded respect, and on top of that, he was known as the toughest guy at Vickroy High. His teammates described him as someone that you wouldn't want to meet in a dark alley.

"I see y'all ain't waste no time waiting for us. Which one is our waitress?" Ryan Days said, looking toward all of the waitresses at the bar.

"Brunette with the glasses," Sean said pointing.

"The brunette! Perfect. That's one of Central Catholic's cheerleaders, she's cute," EJ said.

"Here we go. This guy swears he's a ladies' man," Jimmy said, laughing.

"Come on, man. I'm just a nice guy. Here she comes now," EJ said, smiling.

"Hi, I'm Kelly. You guys ready to order?"

"Yeah, can I get twenty mild wings with blue cheese and a Coke to drink?" Ryan Days said.

"You go to Central, right?" EJ asked.

"Yup, how'd you know?"

"I've seen you cheering. I never forget a pretty face," EJ said.

"Aw, thanks, yes, I cheer. And your name is…" she asked while blushing and giggling.

"I'm EJ, and this is Sean, Jimmy, Tim, Jeremy, Days, and Brandon."

"Well, nice to meet you guys. Now do you know what you wanna order, EJ?"

"Oh, yeah, let me get the same as Days. Twenty mild wings with blue cheese but let me get a Shirley Temple to drink instead," EJ said.

"Okay, guys, I'll go put your order in, and I'll be right back with your drinks," she said with a smile.

"Man, you're nonstop. She was feeling you, though, so I'll give you that," Jimmy said, laughing as the waitress walked away.

"Of course she was, bro," EJ said with a confident smile.

The guys hung out at the G Bar eating wings, talking football, flirting with waitresses, and singing karaoke until about 9:00 p.m. Coach Thomas believed that this type of camaraderie was a necessary component of a championship team, so he encouraged them to hang out outside of school as much as possible. The team genuinely liked one another, so it just came naturally for them. Most of the guys had been playing together since their freshman year, except for Ryan Days. Days transferred to Vickroy a year before, after his parents shipped him off to live with his grandparents because he got into too many fights at his last school. He was from the inner city, but he was a good kid. He just had a chip on his shoulder and wouldn't take anything from anyone. Which made him a heck of a running back but also caused him to get into a lot of trouble.

As the night was winding down, and the guys were leaving, Kelly came over to give everyone their receipts and slipped EJ her phone number.

"Did she just give you her number?" Jimmy asked.

"Yeah, man, I had that in the bag from the start."

"You kill me, man. A Central Catholic cheerleader, huh? Sounds like trouble, bro," Jimmy said, laughing.

"Don't sweat it. I won't start any trouble, man, I promise."

EJ wasn't really a troublemaker, but he was cocky and always seemed to be involved in some type of feud over a girl. He had a weakness for girls and just could not help himself when it came to hitting on the girls from other schools. He got a kick out of making the athletes from the other school jealous, it was psychological warfare for him.

The next day in school, all everyone talked about was the party that Samantha was having after the game on Friday. Vickroy was favored to win states; they had arguably the best player in the country, and it was the first big party of the year.

At lunch, Jimmy, EJ, and Tim Hall all sat together going over the game plan for the game on Friday.

"Remember, bro, if it's two high safeties and the corners are playing off, its cover four. They always press when they run cover two, we can target the middle of the field on that," Jimmy said to EJ.

"Got it. Man, we're gonna hang fifty on these dudes. And after the game, it's really goin' down at Samantha's house."

"Man, stay focused. We don't overlook anyone. We focus on taking care of East Liberty first, and then we can talk about the party. But honestly, I'm not thinking about it until after the game," Jimmy said.

"That's not what you told Samantha. We heard you in the hallway earlier when she walked by, 'Looking forward to Friday night,'" Tim Hall said, mocking Jimmy.

"Yeah, I was talking about the game," Jimmy said, laughing.

"Yeah right. Well, I'm inviting Kelly from the G Bar, so I'm definitely looking forward to having a good night myself," EJ said.

"Well, if we don't get this win, none of us will be going to the party, so first things first," said Jimmy.

"I got you, Captain. You're right," EJ replied.

Vickroy had a good week of practice. They came to practice every day ready to work and practiced with the enthusiasm and intensity that Coach Thomas expected from them. Great teams aren't just an ensemble of talent, they have something more, and Vickroy had "it." Getting a large group of young men committed to focus and work hard to achieve a goal takes a belief in one another that is not found in most teams. They had that special combination of excellent players and coaches, and when they stepped on the field, it was evident that they were all on a mission to do something remarkable.

CHAPTER 2

Going Bad

On Friday morning, Jimmy woke up early to head out to the field to get some pregame mental reps. He liked to go on the field and visualize himself making plays and leading his team to victory before the game. It was something that he heard all the greats did. It also helped him improve his reaction time on the field and gave him confidence in his ability to make game-changing plays.

After he left the field, he went straight into the athletic trainer's room to get water and electrolyte fluids so he'd be well hydrated for the game. While he was in the training room, Coach Thomas walked in.

"Lawson."

"What's up, Coach?"

"Nothin', trying to prepare myself for this damn pep rally. You know how much I hate these things. I want my guys focused on the game."

"I know, Coach. It will be fine. We'll be locked in," Jimmy said, laughing.

"What time does it start again?"

"Second period. So ten."

"All right. I'll see you there," Coach Thomas said as he shook his head and walked out.

Vickroy had a pep rally for every home game during the football season. Most of the players didn't care for all of the extra attention, but they all liked the pep rallies because it got them out of class for an hour.

For the most part, Vickroy's pep rallies weren't different than any others schools. All of the students went to the gym, the band played, the cheerleaders cheered, and there was always some type of battle-of-the-classes challenge. But what made Vickroy's pep rallies unique was the enthusiasm and passion the students had for its football team.

Pep Rally

When the football team was introduced, the students went crazy, as if they were at a pop star's concert. The football team was held in high reverence at Vickroy, and most of the star players were genuinely liked by most of their classmates. They had a good group of guys on the team, and everyone in the school was supportive of their quest for a state title.

After all of the starters were introduced, the cheerleaders performed a routine, the band played the school fight song, and Coach Thomas gave remarks on the season. Coach Thomas wasn't a rah-rah guy, but he knew that the Vickroy athletic director liked all of the excitement, so he played along.

To end the pep rally, the school always did some type of competition between classes called Clash of the Classes. This year's competition was football toss, where a student from each class tried to throw a football into the basketball hoop from half-court. The competitions usually came down to juniors vs. seniors, but this year, the sophomores won when someone from their class hit the shot on his very first try. After he hit the shot, Coach Thomas and all of the football players ran over to congratulate him and started asking him to try out for the team next year. The pep rally was all good fun for the school and was a good way to increase morale, but after it was over, it was time for the team to get focused for the game.

East Liberty Game

As the team walked through the tunnel under the stadium stands, all you could hear was the sound of cleats *click-clacking* on the cement, along with the school band playing out on the field. Coach Thomas noticed that his team was quiet, but he was hoping that it was just a sign of focus and not a sign that they were underestimating their opponent. East Liberty went 5–5 and didn't put up much of a fight in its week 6 matchup versus Vickroy in the previous season, but Coach Thomas expected them to be a little more motivated this year with a new fiery head coach at the helm.

As the team ran out of the tunnel, the fourteen thousand Patriot fans in attendance stood to their feet and cheered as the band played on. The atmosphere on Friday nights at Vickroy High Stadium was cosmic. The band, the cheerleaders, the mascot, the fans, and a team lead by one of the top recruits in the nation made that stadium the place to be on Friday nights in the little Pennsylvania town of New Crofton. Just minutes before kickoff, the energy was overflowing, and Jimmy was ready to feed off of it and put on a show. His confidence was so high that he didn't even get nervous before the games anymore. He looked at every game as an opportunity to prove to the world that he was the best high school player in the nation as a junior. As Jimmy, Sean, Brandon, and Jeremy walked out to midfield for the coin toss, the Vickroy crowd began to chant, "It's all over, it's all over," before the coin flip.

Vickroy won the coin toss and elected to receive. As the captains walked back to the sideline, the rest of the team rushed out to meet them on the field, as their emotional leader, Jeremy Rowley, got in the middle of the huddle.

"Get hype! Get hype! Listen up! From the first whistle to the last, we hit hard and play fast. Set the tone on this return and knock somebody on their butts. *Leave no—freaking—doubt, boys*! Return team, give me a house call on three! One, two, three!"

"House call!"

Coach Thomas looked at Jimmy as he and EJ went back deep to receive the kick and said, "Take it to the crib." Jimmy just looked back at him, pounded his chest, and jogged out on the field.

In the previous week, Merryville was smart enough not to kick or punt the ball to Jimmy, but Coach Thomas knew that East Liberty's coach was too prideful to kick away from him. Just as the kick-off team got set to kick, Coach Thomas whispered to himself, "Make him pay, Deuce."

East Liberty kicked the ball deep right to Jimmy, just as Coach Thomas thought. Jimmy caught the ball at about the two-yard line and took off. He ran the ball straight up the gut, picking up big blocks as he burst through the wedge. When he got to about midfield, he had one guy left to beat and began to high step straight toward him. As the defender broke down to make the tackle, Jimmy gave him a juke and a jump cut that made the defender fall down before he even got a hand on Jimmy. He then accelerated and sprinted to the end zone with no one within ten yards of him.

The stadium erupted as the band played their touchdown celebration song, and Coach Thomas held up one finger, signaling that he wanted to kick the extra point.

Everyone in the stadium knew that it was going to be a long night for East Liberty if they didn't stay away from number 2 at all costs.

When East Liberty got the ball, they attempted to establish a run game by running the ball on first and second down, but strong safety Tim Hall came downhill on both plays to make tackles for no gain. On third down, East Liberty came out in a shotgun trips formation. As soon as the ball was snapped, Jeremy came right up the middle on a blitz and put a punishing hit on the quarterback for the sack.

On fourth down, they were smart enough not to let Jimmy get another return, so they punted the ball out of bounds. As the Vickroy offense took the field for the first time, the crowd went silent in anticipation of the explosion that everyone expected to witness from the offense. Sean looked to the sideline to get the play from Coach Thomas and then took a knee in the middle of the huddle.

"All right, fellas, it's showtime. We goin' gun left 23 power, gun left 23 power on 2. Ready."

"Break!"

On the first snap, Days took the handoff, broke a tackle at the line of scrimmage, bounced outside, and was pushed out of bounds at the fifty-yard line after a gain of eighteen. It was already obvious that East Liberty was in over their heads, and they knew it. The next play was much like the first as Days took another handoff and ran straight up the middle for a fifteen-yard gain.

East Liberty's coach was known for being aggressive on defense and was visibly frustrated as Vickroy continued to pound the ball down into the red zone with ease. Coach Thomas anticipated a blitz on the next play, so he called a wide receiver screen.

When they came to the line of scrimmage, Sean could tell that a blitz was coming because East Liberty's middle linebacker began inching up closer and closer during the cadence.

Sean got the snap and quickly threw it outside to Jimmy. Jimmy caught the ball, made the cornerback miss with a sharp spin move, and sprinted up the hash with a convoy of linemen leading the way en route to his second score of the night.

Down to a quick fourteen-to-nothing deficit, East Liberty came out on their next drive aggressive. They were looking to get back in the game quick and do it via the passing attack. They came out in shotgun four wide receiver sets on their first three plays and picked up consecutive first downs on each of them. On the following first down, they attempted to catch the defense off guard by running a draw, but Jeremy sniffed it out early and made a tackle for no gain. On second down, East Liberty's quarterback dropped back to throw but didn't have much time before Vickroy's D-line was in the backfield, bringing him down for the sack. On third and fifteen near midfield, Jimmy knew that East Liberty would be looking to pass it downfield to pick up the first down and keep the drive that started out promising going. Vickroy's defense came out in its traditional cover 2 shell, but at the snap of the ball, they dropped into a cover 1 blitz, with Jimmy playing the deep middle of the field. The quarterback was under pressure immediately and heaved it up to his receiver on the outside, running a go route, but the ball hung in the air just a little too long. Jimmy got a jump on the throw, made a beeline to the sideline, and jumped over everyone to make the interception. As he came down, he displayed his incredible athleticism by tiptoeing the sideline to stay in bounds and then accelerated across field, leaving the East Liberty receiver in a dust. After the rest of the defense made some big blocks, Jimmy hit the sideline and coasted to the end zone for his third touchdown of the night. Once he crossed the goal line, Jimmy took a knee and said a prayer, pointed to the sky, and then celebrated with his teammates.

Jimmy was really putting on a show, and what was most impressive was how easy he made it look. He scored on offense, defense, and special teams. There was nothing he couldn't do on the football field.

Going into halftime, Vickroy was up 31–0 after Days scored a touchdown on a fifty-yard run, and Vickroy kicked a field goal as time expired in the second quarter.

The third quarter was much like the first two, with Vickroy scoring another two touchdowns on pass plays in which Sean connected with EJ on a sixty-five-yard bomb and a quick slant that EJ took to the house for forty yards.

In the final quarter, Coach Thomas took out most of the starters and ran the clock out as much as possible. With the clock winding down, and as the Vickroy sideline began to celebrate, the crowd started to chant, "We want Central."

The win for Vickroy was not a surprise at all, but the forty-eight-point shutout was another statement game for a team looking to get national recognition and a state championship. The dominant performance by Jimmy early in the game made everyone there to witness a believer. He was the best player on the field by far and maybe the best in the nation.

As the two teams met in the middle of the field to shake hands, a local newspaper reporter tapped Jimmy on the shoulder to get an interview.

"Another impressive win for your team and another impressive individual performance. What message are you guys trying to send to everyone out there?"

"Well, honestly we just wanna come out every week and play well. We work hard all off season and practice hard all week each week, and we expect it to show on the field on Friday nights. We want to be respected as a true state championship contender, but that's not really our concern."

"Three touchdowns in the first half, each in different phases of the game. That's special, how do you make it look so effortless."

"Well, it's probably not as easy as it looks, but that was my personal goal coming into the game tonight because I want the college scouts to see that

I'm a versatile player. I worked my butt off all off season, and it's paying off out there," Jimmy said, smiling.

"That pick six was spectacular, do you plan on playing offense or defense on the next level?"

"Thanks. Like I said, when I'm out there on the field, I know that I train harder and more frequent than my opponent. That's why I'm the best on the field on both sides of the ball. If the school that I choose wants to maximize my talent, they'll let me play both ways. But we'll see. I still got unfinished business on the high school level."

"Thanks for your time, Jimmy, I'll let you go celebrate with your teammates."

"Thanks."

As Jimmy walked to the locker room, an assistant coach for East Liberty tapped Jimmy on the shoulder to get his attention.

"Lawson, great game, man. I've been coaching high school ball for fifteen years, and you're the best I've ever seen. Keep it up, man."

"Thanks," Jimmy said as they shook hands.

When Jimmy got into the locker room, the team already had the music blasting, celebrating another convincing victory. For this team, regular season wins were expected, but it still felt good for them to take another step in the direction of getting another shot at a state title.

As Jimmy sat by his locker, taking off his shoulder pads, Sean slapped him on his thigh and, "Good game, man, it's all paying off," referring to the hard work that Jimmy had been putting in lately. He knew that he was witnessing a combination of talent and work ethic that was going to lead to special things.

"Deuce!" EJ yelled from across the locker room. "Now that we handled business, I'm about to go handle my business at this party!"

"No doubt, text Samantha and ask her what time she wants us to come through," Jimmy said, smiling.

"I'm already ahead of you, bro, I'm waiting for her to hit me back now," EJ said.

"Cool. Let me know what she says, I gotta go home first," Jimmy said as he walked toward the showers. Before he made it to the shower, Coach Thomas turned the radio down and got the teams attention with a whistle.

"Gentlemen, good win tonight. We didn't play perfect, but we played hard, and we were disciplined for the most part, and it showed on the scoreboard. Congratulations on taking another step toward your goal. Celebrate but don't be stupid. Enjoy it tonight, you deserve it, but it's back to work tomorrow. Film at 9:00 a.m."

As Coach Thomas walked back out of the locker room, the team turned the music back up and continued to celebrate as they got showered and changed.

While Jimmy was in the shower, EJ popped in and said, "Yo, she said come through whenever, people are already there."

"Okay, cool. I'm gonna have Sean take me home, and I'll meet y'all over there. Text me when you're on your way," Jimmy replied.

"All right. I gotta go pick up that girl Kelly that we met at the G Bar, and then I'll be over," EJ said.

"All right, man, I'll see you over there," Jimmy said, laughing.

When Jimmy got out of the shower, he got a text from Emily.

Great game Jimmy! You guys were awesome out there tonight

Thanks Em

Delivered

Once Jimmy got dressed, Sean took him home so that he could change before they went over to Samantha's house for the party. When they got to Samantha's house, they could hear the music playing and the sound of a party going on. Sean knocked on the door a few times, but no one answered.

"Let's go around back, man, I think everyone is out back," Jimmy said.

When they got around back, they saw the party already in full effect with music blasting, people dancing, drinking, and playing beer pong. A few guys from the team were already there, sitting at a table drinking beers. "What's up, fellas?" Jimmy said as he walked up to the table where Days and Brandon were sitting.

"What's up, bro?" said Days and Brandon.

"How you feeling, man? You sore? You had a lot of touches tonight," said Brandon.

"Yeah, I'm good, man. I iced up, took some ibuprofen, so I'm straight," Jimmy replied.

"Cool. We need you healthy for this state championship, bro. No need to stay in when we up by three or four touchdowns," Ryan Days said.

"You're right, but you know I don't like coming out," Jimmy said.

"Yeah, but—" Sean said, but in midsentence, Samantha yelled, "Jimmy!" as she ran up to him to give him a big hug.

"I'm so glad you came!" she said in excitement.

"Yeah, she been asking about you since we got here," Ryan Days said.

"Oh my god, no, I have not! I asked about you once!" she said, laughing.

"It's all good, you can ask about me as much as you want. Don't worry about him," Jimmy said.

"Come on, guys, take a picture with me for my Snap," Samantha said.

The guys all got up to take a picture with Samantha. "Are your parents out of town?" Jimmy asked after everyone sat back down.

"Yup, they won't be back until Sunday night."

"Oh cool, your neighbors won't snitch on you for having a party?" Jimmy asked.

"No, because my parents don't care as long we keep it out in the yard. They just don't want people in the house destroying things."

"Oh yeah? That's dope. My mom wouldn't be having it at all," Jimmy said.

"Come inside with me," Samantha said as she grabbed his hand and pulled him toward the door."

"Aight, I'll be right back, guys."

"No, he won't," Samantha said as they walked in the house. The rest of the guys looked at one another, shrugged, and laughed.

"Do you want a drink?" Samantha asked.

"Yeah, I'll take a beer," Jimmy replied.

"Okay, I got Blue Moon or Natty Ice. Which one?" she asked as she looked in the refrigerator.

"Let me get that Blue Moon."

"Okay, you're not driving, are you?"

"Nah, Sean drove but I'm not trying to get hammered anyway. Got workouts in the morning."

"Okay, cool. Sit down. I wanted you to come inside with me because it's less crazy in here, and I want to ask you something."

"What's up?" Jimmy said as they sat on the couch.

"Is Emily Jennings your girlfriend?"

"No, we're just friends. Why?"

"Because someone told me that you're taking her to the homecoming dance and that you guys are dating."

"Well, I haven't decided if I'm even going to homecoming, and no, that's not my girl," Jimmy said, smiling.

"Well, that's good to know," Samantha said as she got closer.

"Why is that?"

"Because I wanna be your girl," Samantha said as she moved in for a kiss.

As soon as they began kissing, Sean came running in the backdoor. "Jimmy! Get out here, man. We got a problem," he yelled.

"What's wrong?" Jimmy asked as he got up from the couch and started walking back outside. When he got out to the yard, he saw EJ, Days, and Brandon talking, and they were all visibly upset. As he got closer, he noticed that EJ's clothes were dirty, and he was bleeding from his nose and mouth. "What the hell happened, man?" Jimmy asked as everyone at the party looked on.

"Man, I went to pick up that girl Kelly, and when I got to her house, these Central dudes was outside, talkin', trash. I wasn't gonna take it there, but the one dude kicked my car, so I socked him. Then they jumped me," EJ said.

"How many of 'em was it? Did you recognize any of them?" Jimmy asked.

"It was about four or five of 'em, man. Only one I recognized was the dude Boomer, their middle linebacker."

"Aight, let's go, we goin' back over there right now!" Days said in a matter-of-fact tone.

"Hold up, man, calm down. First of all, are you good, EJ?" Jimmy said as he scanned EJ up and down to see how badly he was hurt.

"I'm all right, they only got a few good licks on me, and then they ran because some lady came outside and said she was calling the cops. Brandon, come back over there with me and Days, bro."

"If y'all are goin' back over there, me and Sean are coming with you," Jimmy said.

"Nah, Deuce, we'll handle it. Don't need you to be getting in trouble with us," Ryan Days said.

"I'm not letting y'all go over there without me," Jimmy said.

"All right, we out then. Follow me. It's over off of Southern Parkway," EJ said as they all walked toward their cars.

When they got over to Kelly's house, the New Crofton Police were outside, and none of the Central players were in sight. As they drove by, the lady that called the police recognized EJ's car and pointed it out to the officers. The officers then flagged down the car that EJ was driving and had him pull over to talk to him. When Sean and Jimmy saw EJ being pulled over by the police, they turned around and went home because they wanted to avoid any police contact.

"EJ, what happened over here earlier?" the officer asked.

"I don't know, sir, we were just driving by on our way home."

"Don't lie to me, man. The lady said she saw you over here fighting earlier and said you got in this car and took off when she told you she was calling the police."

"Well, some guys jumped me, but I'm okay. We were just driving home from another party, sir." EJ said in a very nonpersuasive tone.

"You got jumped, huh? And you rallied the troops to come back to retaliate. I saw Jimmy and Sean driving in the other car. Look, you guys just played a great game and got too much going for you to mess it up by doing something stupid. Get the hell out of here, and I don't even wanna see you in this neighborhood no more. You don't live around here, you got no business in this neighborhood. If I see you in this neighborhood again, I'm locking you up for disturbing the peace."

"Yes, sir, thank you, sir," EJ said as he rolled up his window and slowly drove off.

The next morning, before the team went in to start the film session, Coach Thomas called Jimmy, Sean, and EJ into his office.

"What happened last night?" Coach Thomas said in a frustrated tone.

The three players all looked at one another in shock and confusion. They were all wondering the same thing, how did he know something happened? "Don't be shocked, Officer Roberson called me first thing this morning, and told me y'all were at some party, fighting," he said.

"Well, technically we weren't at a party fighting," Jimmy said.

"All right, so what were y'all doing?"

"Look, Coach, Jimmy and Sean didn't have anything to do with it. I went to this girl's house to take her to a party, and these Central guys jumped me. I didn't start it," EJ said.

"But all of y'all went back over there to finish it, huh?"

"It wasn't like that, Coach. We just went back over there to see who it was," said Sean.

"Y'all think I'm an idiot? I expect y'all to be the leaders of this team and put the team first. I'm all about defending your teammates, but to go back over there after the fact is just asking for trouble. If they were Central players like you say, we're gonna make them pay for this on the field. But as far as this off-field stuff, we're done. I'm gonna call their coach and make sure he's telling them the same thing. We're gonna settle this on the field. Are we clear?"

"Yes, sir," they all replied.

When Jimmy got back home, while lying on the couch, watching college football, he got a text from Samantha.

What happened last night???? Are you guys ok???

> Yeah i'm sorry we left like that

Did you find the guys??

> No someone called the cops

😊 did you guys get in trouble??

> Haha no we didn't do anything
>
> Delivered

Lol ok jus checking. So before we were so rudely interrupted last night 😊, I wanted to ask you about homecoming. Are you going???

> I dunno. I really don't wanna ask my mom for money to buy a outfit and all that. And I just need to make sure I'm able to focus on the game that week. I don't want u to wait on my decision, if someone else asks u to go I won't be mad at u

Well I'm not goin with anybody else but you better not either 😊. Hopefully I'll see you there

> Deal. I got u
>
> Delivered

Jimmy wanted to go to the homecoming dance, but he didn't want all of the distractions that would come along with asking a girl out and planning everything. He wanted to focus on football and didn't want to think about the dance until after they won the game. Football was everything to Jimmy, and he wouldn't be able to enjoy the homecoming dance if they lost the game, so he had to make the game the priority.

CHAPTER 3

─── ❧ ───

Whoa

The next few games against Joppatowne High School, Coldspring High School, and Eisenhower High School were a breeze. Vickroy dominated and won those games by a combined score of 113–23. Everyone was still healthy, and the team was clicking on all cylinders. They were playing with focus and attention to detail even against substantially inferior opponents. They weren't playing down to their competition, they came out each game and executed their game plan and kept their foot on the gas until the game clock struck all zeroes. Jimmy was leading the state in all-purpose yards and touchdowns with 1,217 yards and sixteen respectively. Vickroy was ranked number 2 in the state rankings for Class 4A and was expected to win the remaining games on their schedule, but ranked just ahead of them at number 1 was their cross-town rivals, New Crofton Central Catholic.

Central Catholic had been to the last three state championship games and won two out of the three. They had beaten Vickroy in the state playoffs the previous season and were favorites to win another state title this year. They also had Kevin Jones, a 210-pound running back with legitimate 4.3 speed. He was Central Catholic's do-everything player and was rated as the top player in the country. He had already made a verbal commitment to attend the University of Georgia and was on pace to break his own state record of forty-eight rushing TDs in a season. He was the total package: he had elite speed, great vision, elusive moves, and he ran angry. In last year's play-off matchup, he embarrassed the Vickroy defense running for 399 yards and five touchdowns. He was the only player standing in the way of Jimmy being named player of the year this season. They both were equally impressive individually, and it seemed that the deciding factor would be the success of their teams. Leading your team to a state title was a major consideration for the organizations that awarded those accolades and also for college recruiters that were always looking for little things that separated one top prospect from another.

In addition to Jones, they also had All-American senior quarterback Adam Sanchez and All-American senior linebacker Charles "Boomer" Hicks. These guys were considered three of the top 100 players in the country, and none of them were interested in finishing high school without winning another state title in their senior year. Sanchez was ranked as the number 12 dual-threat quarterback in the country, and he was committed to Ohio State University. Boomer Hicks was physically imposing and intimidating. He was a hard hitter with a head that seemed to be made of iron. He was ranked as the number 8 inside linebacker in the country and was committed to Louisiana State University.

Central Catholic was a private school, so they didn't have to follow the same school zone rules as the other schools in the district. This allowed them to recruit their athletes from all over the county, so their teams were stacked with some of the best players in the state every year. The best players from all over the state would transfer to Central Catholic to have an opportunity to compete for a state title and get national recognition.

Outside of the three All-Americans, they also had seven other players that were all-state selections in the previous season, some of which were likely to receive All-American honors this season. The team didn't have any weaknesses, and that included coaching. They weren't just an all-star ensemble of talent, they also played hard and were a disciplined bunch. During the previous season's state championship run, they proved that they were a mentally tough team as well. They got behind in a few games and were able to battle back to pull out victories. That experience was important because if they were to get down again at some point, they wouldn't be discouraged because they had been there before. They were big, strong, and played physical, and for any team to beat them, they would have to outplay them for four quarters.

Most of the Vickroy and Central Catholic players grew up together and played Little League together. The best ones got recruited to go to Central Catholic and offered scholarship money to help pay for the private school tuition. Everyone else went to Vickroy. Because of that, the Central Catholic kids always thought that they were better than Vickroy kids and expected to beat them every year. They had a cocky attitude that was just annoying. Even the kids that weren't athletes were arrogant because most of them were privileged kids from well-off families and were used to having the best things given to them. Everyone who was a fan of Vickroy was so excited because they knew that this was an opportunity to knock the Central fans off of their high horses and humble them a little bit.

Homecoming

The next week was homecoming week for Vickroy. There were a lot of school festivities for homecoming week that included the football game on Friday night and the homecoming dance on Saturday. During homecoming week, the cheerleaders went all out. They decorated each of the starting player's lockers and designated an entire hallway to each of the team's captains with more elaborate decorations. On top of that, they also went out to all of the senior's homes and decorated them from top to bottom for game day. These traditions made New Crofton kids dream about growing up to play high school football at Vickroy and made proud parents out of those that could say their son was a Patriot.

Typically Coach Thomas tried his best to schedule a subpar team for homecoming to guarantee a victory, but this year, Vickroy had to face perennial playoff contender St Martins High in the homecoming game. St. Martins didn't have the talent that Vickroy had this year, but they were not to be underestimated or overlooked. St. Martins played tough, and the games were close every year, regardless of talent. If Vickroy took them lightly, St. Martins would be sure to make them pay for it.

The team practiced hard all week and were focused. They couldn't afford to lose this late in the year and jeopardize their playoff chances. The expectations for this season were way too high for that type of letdown.

Homecoming Game: St. Martin's High School

Coach Thomas addressed the team in the locker room before the game.

"All right, men, we know what we gotta do. I've been telling you all week to be prepared for a dog fight. This team is not gonna be intimidated, and they're not gonna roll over for you. Come out fast, punch them in the mouth, and keep your foot on their necks until it's over. We gotta be physical up front, and we gotta tackle on defense. Make sure you're wrapping up. Offense, execute the plays. Don't try to do too much, just execute. Dominate the man in front of you. We take care of those things, and we'll keep this train rolling. We got a packed house. Your families, classmates, alumni, fans, media, and college scouts are all here watching. Let's give 'em a show. Bring it in. Dominate on three. One, two, three."

"Dominate."

As Vickroy ran out of the tunnel through the artificial smoke, you could already feel the electricity in the stadium. It was as if the fans had already began celebrating the homecoming victory before the game even started. The team's energy was high, and they were ready to deliver an unforgettable homecoming performance.

As the captains went to the center of the field for the coin toss, the Patriot mascot sprinted up and down the sideline, waving the school flag and entertaining the rambunctious fans.

St. Martin's won the coin toss and elected to receive the kickoff.

Coach Thomas yelled to the team as he walked down the sideline, "All right, the defense is up first. Set the tone!"

Vickroy lined up and kicked the ball deep out of the back of the end zone. As Jimmy and the rest of the defense jogged out on the field, Sean yelled to Jimmy, "Deuce, if the ball is in the air, it's yours, baby."

Jimmy yelled back, "My rock."

On the first play, St. Martin's lined up in a spread formation, handed the ball off to the running back, and was stopped immediately at the line of scrimmage. On the next play, they stayed in the spread formation and threw a slant to the inside receiver, but it was broken up. On third down, they came out in empty, snapped the ball, and the quarterback took off up the middle on a QB draw. St. Martin's quarterback was a legitimate running threat, and it looked for a second as if he would have enough room to get the first down, but the Vickroy defense was swarming. Jeremy, Mike, and Jimmy converged on the quarterback in a hurry and stopped him about two yards short of the first down. After the tackle, Jimmy looked at the first down marker, saw that the ball was short of the line to gain, got up, and threw his fist up to signal it was fourth down. The defense was off to a strong start, and the high-powered offense was about to get the opportunity to follow suit.

Jimmy lined up deep to return the punt, but like every other team Vickroy had faced, St. Martin's was smart enough to not test Jimmy's dangerous return ability, so they punted it out of bounds around the Vickroy forty-yard line.

The offense ran out on the field and got in the huddle. Sean got on a knee in the middle of the huddle to call the play.

"All right, fellas, let's take care of business on this drive. We got I slot left 23 power. Ready."

"Break."

The offense got to the line of scrimmage and got set. As Sean went under the center, he surveilled the defense and noticed the linebackers and safeties creeping up, telegraphing a blitz. He immediately called an audible to a play action bootleg.

Sean signaled the audible by grabbing his face mask, "Fido, Fido, Fido, Fido. Set, hike!"

The center snapped the ball, Sean faked the handoff to Days, and sprinted out to his right. The entire St. Martin's defense bit on the run fake and were completely out of position to defend the pass. Sean looked downfield, saw EJ running wide open on the deep crossing pattern, and let it fly. EJ caught the ball in stride and high-stepped his way to the end zone on their first offensive play of the game. "Too easy, too easy!" EJ said as his team joined him in the end zone to celebrate.

The homecoming crowd was going crazy after their team had jumped out to a quick 7–0 lead only three minutes into the game.

On St. Martin's next possession, they came out in a double tight end I formation and was able to slowly move the ball down the field with short runs up the middle by the fullback. St. Martin's head coach knew they needed to slow the game down to have any chance in the game, so his plan was to control the clock and play keep-away as much as possible. This was a strategy to limit the number of possessions that Vickroy would get in an attempt to keep them from scoring as many points as they had been all season.

Vickroy's defense was playing well, but St. Martin's had a monstrous offensive line, and they were blowing the Vickroy defensive line off the ball every play.

They marched the ball down the field, eating up most of the clock in the first quarter, and scored a touchdown. It was 7–7, and the Vickroy defense was frustrated.

The Vickroy offense took the field and didn't have any trouble moving the ball down the field. On their next possession, they were able to put together a nine-play drive and scored a touchdown on a short pass to Days where he came out of the backfield, caught the ball on the sideline, made one defender miss, and dragged another for about three yards on his way to the end zone.

Vickroy had retaken the lead, but it was time for the defense to go out on the field and get a stop. When the St. Martin's offense got back out on the field, they came out in a double tight end I formation that they were using all game and started the ground-and-pound attack once again. Just like on their last drive, they were able to get three yards, four yards, three yards, and then a first down consistently. This didn't only chew up the clock and kept Vickroy's explosive offense off the field, but also it was demoralizing to the Vickroy defense. They knew what was coming, and they couldn't stop it. They were getting discouraged on the defensive side of the ball, and the offense was beginning to feel the pressure of feeling like they needed to score on every possession to keep pace. St. Martin's drove down again and scored to make the score 14–14 with about four minutes remaining in the half.

When Vickroy got back on offense, they were desperate to get another touchdown before the end of the half. They came out in a spread formation and started the drive with a screen pass to Days. Days caught the ball and made one defender miss but was tackled for a short gain. On the next play, Sean tried to force the ball to Jimmy on a corner route, but he was double-covered and had to turn into a defender to prevent the interception. On third down, Sean was able to scramble to pick up the first down but wasn't able to get out of bounds to stop the clock before the two-minute warning. In the huddle, Sean tried to motivate his team to get points before the end of the half.

"We need to get six on this drive, fellas. This game is too close for comfort. Let's turn it up. We're goin' gun empty strong right 959 X cross Y post. On two, on two, ready."

"Break."

When they broke the huddle, Sean went behind center and surveilled the defense. He saw that the defense was clearly playing deep to prevent the deep pass. When the ball was snapped, Sean saw the shallow crossing pattern open up immediately but wanted to take a shot at the deep pass. He attempted to look the safety off and threw it deep to EJ, who was running a fade down the right sideline. As soon as he let the ball go, the St. Martin's safety broke on the ball and made a pretty exceptional play as he was able to drag his foot to stay in bounds while lunging to make the interception.

St. Martin's took over on their own fifteen-yard line with about a minute and forty-five seconds left on the clock before halftime. Their offense came on the field and played it conservative, running the ball three straight downs to run the clock out.

As the half ended, the stadium had definitely gotten more quiet, and most of the Vickroy players had their heads down, as if they were losing the game. It was 14–14 going into halftime, but they weren't used to being in close games. They had been winning by multiple touchdowns in the first half of every game of the season so far. This was their first test of the season, but it was good that it was coming now in the regular season to prepare them for a playoff run.

When they got into the locker room, tensions were high, and the guys were starting to panic. The offense started blaming the defense, and the defense blamed the offense for not getting points before the end of the half.

After the coaches were done going over the halftime adjustments, Coach Thomas walked over to Jimmy and said, "It's time for you to take this game over."

"You know what, Coach, I was just thinking the same thing," Jimmy replied with a smile as they gave each other a pound. Jimmy wasn't overwhelmed by the adversity; he was waiting for an opportunity like this to show everyone what he was made of. There were a lot of talented players in the country, but this was his chance to prove that he had something in him that was special. Something that you didn't find in all good athletes.

Vickroy was receiving the ball at the start of the second half, and they needed to score a touchdown, or they would be in jeopardy of letting the game slip away.

As the kickoff and kick return teams got set, Jimmy went back deep to prepare to return the kick. He was hoping St. Martin's would give him an opportunity to return the kick, but they squib-kicked the ball low and short to prevent a return by Jimmy.

On the first play of the drive, Coach Thomas didn't hesitate to get the ball in the hands of his best player. Vickroy lined up in a double tight end single back formation. At the snap of the ball, Sean pitched the ball to Days on a toss going right. As the defense began to pursue Days, Jimmy came back around, and Days handed it to him on the reverse, going back to the left side of the defense. With all of the St. Martin's players on the right side of the field, Jimmy had nothing but daylight as he sprinted down the left sideline with blockers in front of him. He went sixty-five yards untouched, and just like that, Vickroy had retaken the lead only one minute into the second half.

Now the challenge was stopping the power run game that St. Martin's had established in the first half. When St. Martin's got the ball, to no one's surprise, they lined up in the same formation that they had success with in the first half. Coach Thomas decided to go with 5–2 defensive front and send additional pressure up the middle.

On the first play, the adjustment by Coach Thomas proved to be effective as Vickroy was able to stop St. Martin's running back for no gain. On the second play, St. Martin's came out in the same formation but tried to run the ball to the outside, and that was stopped for a short gain as Tim Hall came down in a hurry from the safety position with a big hit on the running back. Now it was third and long, and Vickroy finally had the St. Martin's offense on the ropes. They needed to get a third down stop to protect their lead. St. Martin's stayed in the same formation, and Coach Thomas stayed aggressive by sending pressure, leaving his defensive backs in man-to-man coverage. St. Martin's snapped the ball and attempted to set up a screen to the running back. With the Vickroy linebackers blitzing up the middle, the running back was uncovered, and it looked like St. Martin's had the blocking set up perfectly for a huge gain, but Jimmy had other plans. Jimmy's responsibility was to cover the tight end in man to man, but when he noticed his man and the offensive line setting up to block for the running back, he took a beeline toward the running back from his safety position. As soon as the St. Martin's running back caught the ball, Jimmy was there, but instead of just bringing the ball carrier down, Jimmy ripped the ball from his hands, stiff-armed him to the ground, and took off in the other direction toward the end zone.

As Jimmy raced down the field for his second score of the half, the homecoming crowd went wild. They were back in party mode after their team had just made the play that would likely give Vickroy a big-enough lead to secure the victory.

Jimmy crossed the goal line, turned around and pointed to Coach Thomas on the sideline. Coach Thomas asked him to take the game over, and that was exactly what he was doing. It was 28–14, and Vickroy had all the momentum on their side.

When St. Martin's got the ball back, they tried to go back to the ground-and-pound strategy, but the adjustment by Vickroy made their running attack ineffective. Vickroy was able to force a three and out and got the ball back with nine minutes left in the third quarter.

When Vickroy got back on offense, Coach Thomas decided to give St. Martin's a taste of their own medicine with a punishing running attack. Play after play, Sean handed the ball off to Days, and they slowly pounded the ball all the way down the field, breaking the will of the St. Martin's defense and chewing up the game clock in the third quarter.

As the third quarter came to a close, Vickroy had a first down on the St. Martin's seventeen-yard line. Vickroy had made it the whole way down the field on thirteen straight running plays, and the St. Martin's defense was exhausted. "Let's take a shot on this next play, Coach," Sean said to Coach Thomas in the huddle.

"All right, let's go I right, 32 yogi, 79 option. But don't force it. If it's there, take it, but if not, just throw it away."

"Got it, Coach."

At the start of the fourth quarter, Vickroy came out of the huddle and lined up in the I formation. They snapped the ball, Sean faked the handoff to Days, and the exhausted St. Martin's defense came up to defend the run. When Sean saw the defense bite on the run fake, he looked up and saw Jimmy running toward the end zone with a defender trailing him by about three yards. Sean threw the ball toward the back pylon, and Jimmy was able to track the ball down, dive, and make the catch while keeping both of his feet in the end zone for the touchdown.

"Stick a fork in 'em, it's a wrap," EJ said while running over to Jimmy to celebrate the touchdown.

As the band played the touchdown celebration song, the players on the Vickroy sideline looked to the home crowd and started celebrating. Vickroy was up 35–14, and St. Martin's was dejected on their sideline. They knew that even if they were able to get their running attack going again, like they did in the first half, stopping the Vickroy offense was not likely.

The two teams exchanged a couple of late touchdowns as the backups came in to get some playing time, and the homecoming game ended with a final score of 42–21. It was another convincing win for Vickroy, and for Coach Thomas, it was great to see them get a victory after overcoming a little adversity.

When Vickroy got into the locker room, all of the players were excited to celebrate at the homecoming dance. They were on a roll, and the homecoming dance was something that they had been looking forward to all season.

As Jimmy took off his equipment, he got a text from Emily.

Congrats on the win! You played amazing as usual. If you're coming to the dance I'll see you there

Hey Em, thanks. Yeah I'll be there.

Make sure u save a dance for me

Delivered

☺ of course I will

Homecoming Dance

The next evening, after Jimmy was done getting dressed for the dance, his mom, Deborah, took pictures of him while he waited for Sean to come pick him up. "What time did Sean say he was getting here?" Deborah asked.

"He was supposed to be here fifteen minutes ago. He's never on time."

"He's gotta make an entrance!" She laughed.

"I guess," Jimmy replied, laughing.

"Why aren't you wearing any socks, Jim?"

"Ma, you don't wear socks with loafers. That's the style."

"Oh, okay, if you say so," she said, rolling her eyes and smiling.

"Come on, Ma, you know I'm fly."

"Okay, whatever. I see Sean's red truck pulling up now," Deborah said, smiling.

"Okay, how do I look?"

"Handsome."

"Smooth. Thanks, Ma, I love you," Jimmy said as he gave her a hug.

"Love you too. Be back by one and let me know when you get in."

"Okay, I will."

"Have fun," Deborah said as Jimmy walked out the door.

"What's up, bro?" Jimmy said as he got in the car.

"What's up, man? I like that jacket."

"Thanks, man, I got this a few months ago. Figured I'd break it out for homecoming. Are we lame for going without dates?"

"Heck no, man. Why go with one date when we can go by ourselves and have a buffet of dates," Sean said, smiling.

"You're right," Jimmy replied, laughing.

"Of course I am. I'm sure Samantha will have you tied down all night, but I'm playing the field tonight, bro."

"Whatever, man," Jimmy said, laughing.

"I just hope this ibuprofen kicks in, so I can get my party on. I rolled my ankle in the game last night. It's still a little swollen."

"I hit the ice bath this morning. That definitely helped."

The guys got to the dance, and when they got inside, the music was playing, the dance floor was packed, and the students were already having a great time. Jimmy and Sean walked around and said what's up to all of their friends and teammates before hitting the dance floor. Now that they were there, the party had officially begun, and everyone was excited. While the guys were out on the dance floor, Jimmy spotted Emily sitting at a table with a few of her friends.

"Yo, I will be right back," he said to Sean as he maneuvered through the crowded dance floor.

"Wow, Em, you look gorgeous!" he said, smiling as he approached her table.

"Well, thank you, you don't look bad yourself. You clean up well," she replied with a smile.

"Thank you, I try. What time did you all get here?"

"My dad dropped us off about an hour ago," one of Emily's friends replied.

"Oh, okay. You guys having fun?" Jimmy asked the girls.

"Yeah, we've just been sitting here talking. We haven't danced much." Emily laughed.

"Okay, anyone want a drink or anything?" Jimmy asked.

"No, we're okay. Thanks for offering," Emily replied.

"Okay, well, you let me know if you need any-thing and make sure you come find me when you're ready for that dance," Jimmy said, smiling at Emily.

"Okay, I will."

"All right, have a good night, ladies. Y'all behave yourselves."

"Bye, Jimmy." They laughed as Jimmy walked away.

Jimmy went to get himself a drink, but on his way to the drinks table, he saw Samantha out on the dance floor, dancing alone.

As he approached her, they made eye contact, and she smiled and started walking toward him as she continued to dance. "Hey, you. I'm glad you finally made it over here to see me," she said.

"I'm sorry, I just got here not too long ago. You know Sean is always fashionably late."

"Well, I'm just glad you're here now," she said with a smile.

Jimmy and Samantha danced and had a good time all night. The gym was packed full of people, but it was like they were the only ones in the room. Neither one of them wanted the night to end. Jimmy had been working so hard at football, along with his schoolwork, so this was a special night for him to enjoy some of the fruits of his labor. As the night came to an end, the homecoming king and queen were crowned by their predecessors, and everyone got to take pictures with the newly crowned royal couple. It was a great night filled with fun and laughter. It was just what the guys on the football team needed to take a break from the stress and pressure of a football season that was filled with very high expectations.

When the dance concluded, Jimmy, Sean, Samantha, and other friends all walked out to their cars in the parking lot together. "Hey, guys, Ashley is having a little kickback at her house next weekend. Of course, you're all invited. I know you guys don't have a game next Friday, so you better be there," Samantha said.

"Word? Yeah, we'll swing through. What time?" Sean asked.

"Around eight or nine. Nothing special. We'll probably just order pizza and hang out."

"Cool. We'll stop by after we leave the Central game. Get home safe, okay?" Jimmy said as he gave Samantha a hug and a kiss.

"Thank you for a great night," she said as she got in the car.

"The pleasure was mine. Text me when you get in."

After Samantha and her friends drove off, Jimmy got in the car with Sean to go home.

"How was your night, bro?" Jimmy asked.

"The night was lit. With you being wifed up all night, I was getting all the love in there." He laughed.

"Yeah, you're lucky I took myself out of the game for the night," he joked.

"Bro, did you see how sad Emily looked?"

"Ah, Emily. I forgot all about Emily. I wanted to at least get a few dances with her," he said with his hands on his forehead in frustration.

"Well, yeah, she was hurt, bro."

"That's my fault, man. I'll text her and apologize."

When Sean dropped Jimmy off at his house, he went in and took a shower. When he got out of the shower, he had a text from Emily.

It wasn't Jimmy's intention to break Emily's heart, but Samantha had his attention, and he was having a good time, letting things blossom with her. He wasn't happy about disappointing Emily, and he didn't want to lose her as a friend, but things were going well with Samantha, and he liked spending time with her. Over all, the guys had a great week and a great night. It was now time to refocus on winning a state title.

CHAPTER 4

—— ❧ ——

99 Problems

After Vickroy's win in the homecoming game, they were off to a 6–0 start and looked unstoppable. But there was one team that looked just as impressive, if not better, and that was Central Catholic. Central had won four of the last seven state championships in Pennsylvania and lost a heartbreaker in last year's championship game by one point on the final play. This year they seemed to be determined to avenge that loss and bring home another title. They were destroying everyone they played and making it look easy.

In the previous week, they beat Merryville 56–0, and the week before that, they beat Coldspring 38–6. It was like every time they played a team that Vickroy played, they made it a point to beat them worse than Vickroy did.

Since Vickroy had a bye, Jimmy, Sean, and EJ all decided to go watch Central play Hamilton on Friday night. Hamilton was usually pretty good and were undefeated so far this season. They were the first team that Central faced all season that actually had a chance of beating them, so everyone was expecting it to be a great game. On top of that, Vickroy was scheduled to play Hamilton in the last game of the regular season and would most likely be seeing Central at some point in the playoffs, so this gave the boys a good opportunity to scout their upcoming opponents.

When they got to the stadium, the first quarter was almost over, and the game was already one-sided. Central had jumped out to a fourteen-point lead and were driving down the field well on their way to another touchdown. As they walked through the stands, everyone knew who they were because they were wearing their varsity letterman jackets. "Yo, Vickroy," a Central student yelled over to the guys. "Y'all can scout all you want, my boys are getting another ring this year."

"We'll see," Jimmy replied with a smile.

Vickroy was confident in their team, but Central was definitely a cause for concern. Central had great athletes, and they played disciplined football. That combination is why they were a football powerhouse, always nationally ranked, and always a favorite to win states year in and year out.

By the end of the first half, Central was up 24–0 with Kevin Jones breaking dazzling runs and showing off his athleticism. One play stood out in particular. Central had the ball on their own thirty-five-yard line, they came out in a spread formation with Jones out at slot receiver. At the snap of the ball, Jones took off vertical and threw his hand up, Sanchez saw that he was covered but let it rip and threw it deep. As soon as the ball went in the air, Jones accelerated and separated as he made the catch and coasted down the sideline to the end zone. It was clear that he was moving at a different speed than anyone else Vickroy had faced, and he was definitely living up to the hype.

Once the second half started, the show continued. Sanchez looked like a man among boys. He had prototype size at 6'4" and 225 pounds and a rocket arm to match. The team was just clicking on all cylinders, and Kevin Jones added another amazing touchdown in the third before retiring for the night. By the fourth quarter, Central was in cruise control with a comfortable 31–0 lead.

As the game began to wind down, Jimmy, Sean, and EJ started to make their way out to beat the crowd, but as they were leaving, a reporter stopped them. "Hey, guys, can I talk to you guys really quick?" he said as he walked over with his tape recorder.

"Sure," Jimmy said, sort of reluctantly.

"Okay, thanks. Central just put on an amazing performance and made a heck of a statement tonight. What did you guys think of it?"

"Well, it was impressive for sure, but we believe if we play our best, there's no high school team in this country that can beat us," Sean replied.

"Jimmy, do you have anything to add?"

"No, we don't wanna take anything away from those guys. They're a great team, they played great tonight. What more can I say?"

"Thanks, guys."

"No problem," Jimmy said as they walked away toward their car.

"Yo, Jimmy. Jones is the real deal, man," EJ said.

"Yeah, did you see the play where he was surrounded by like ten Hamilton guys, and somehow he broke free and ran for a sixty-yard touchdown?" Sean added.

"Yeah, man, I saw it. He is as good as they say. But the season is still young, fellas. We gotta focus on Westview next week. No point of looking ahead. One game at a time," Jimmy said with a smile.

Jimmy was definitely impressed, but a playoff matchup versus Central is what he trained so hard for. He wanted the opportunity to go head-to-head with Kevin Jones to prove that he was just as good, if not better. He was happy to see such a dominant performance by Central. Knowing that this Central team was one of the best in years was going to make a victory over them even more satisfying. There was no doubt that Jimmy was excited about getting a chance to play a team that was clearly heads and shoulders above pretty much everyone in the state, but it didn't seem like his teammates felt the same way. What they just witnessed versus a respectable team had them worried, and it was obvious.

After the Central game, Jimmy and Sean went to Ashley's house to hang out with Samantha and some of their other classmates. When they got there, they were greeted at the door by Samantha. They went inside and went into the basement where there were six of their other classmates just hanging out and watching television.

"Do you guys want a beer or anything?" Ashley asked.

"I'm driving, so nah," Sean said.

"You can have a drink, bro, I'll drive, and you can just stay at my house tonight," Jimmy said.

"Well, in that case, yeah, I'll take a beer," Sean said, laughing.

Everyone stayed at Ashley's house for a few hours, talking, laughing, and playing board games. Some of them had a few beers, but no one got drunk. It was a laid-back night for the most part, and everyone had a good time.

When it was time for everyone to leave, Sean tossed Jimmy the keys to his car.

"Get us home safe, bro."

"Shut up, I drive better than you." Jimmy laughed.

"Pass your test then, chump."

"I'm taking the test next summer, man."

As they drove home, Jimmy decided to take a back road. The back road route was a little faster, but the street was very narrow and windy. As Jimmy drove down the dark windy road, he noticed police activity in the road up ahead.

"Sean, wake up, it's police lights up there. It looks like they're blocking the road."

"It's cool, man, just go around them."

When Jimmy got closer, he saw that the police cars were, in fact, blocking the roadway while they searched a car that they had pulled over. Jimmy slowly approached the police cars to see if there was enough space for him to pass through but was stopped by one of the police officers.

"Good evening, officer, can we get through?" Jimmy asked as he rolled down his window.

"What's up, guys. Where you headed?" the officer asked as he shined his flashlight in the car to see inside.

"We're just headed home, sir."

"You guys had anything to drink tonight?" the officer asked as he looked at Sean.

"No, sir," Jimmy quickly responded.

"All right, let me see your license and registration."

"I don't have my license on me, sir," Jimmy said as he handed the officer the registration from Sean's glove box.

"You don't have your license with you? Okay, step out the car, guys."

When Jimmy and Sean got out of the car, the officers gave them a pat down while they ran their names through the system to check their driving records and criminal history.

"James Lawson…you don't have a driver license? It says you only have a learner's permit…"

"Yes, sir," Jimmy replied in a nervous tone.

"Jimmy?" another officer asked as he approached.

"You know this guy?" the primary officer asked his partner.

"Jimmy Lawson, yeah, I know him. This is Vickroy's dynamic duo. The star quarterback and star receiver. These guys are gonna win a state championship in a couple of months."

"Yeah, well it looks like Sean has been drinking, and Jimmy is driving him around without a license."

"Really, guys? Get in the car and drive straight home. Jimmy, you drive, but if I or any other officer sees you out anywhere else tonight, you'll be spending the weekend in jail," he said in a disappointed and upset tone.

"Yes, sir, thank you, sir," Jimmy and Sean replied as they quickly walked back to the car.

The guys got back in the car and drove straight to Jimmy's house like the officer told them to. They both knew that they dodged a serious bullet. If they had been arrested that night, they would have most likely been suspended from the team for at least a few games and could have possibly jeopardized everything that they had worked so hard for. That experience put things into perspective for both of them. They realized that they had an opportunity to do something great, and that opportunity should not have been taken for granted. They were ready to block out all of the distractions and get ready to finish the season strong.

CHAPTER 5

— ❧ —

Sicko Mode

After Vickroy returned from their bye week, Jimmy seemed more determined than ever. His workouts were more intense, he was more focused in practice, and what he did in the Westview game had everyone on his team in awe and more confident than ever. He was a one-man band accumulating over three hundred all-purpose yards and scoring four touchdowns.

Over the next two weeks, Vickroy continued their undefeated streak and tallied impressive victories versus Highland High and Wheaton High. They won those games by a combined score of 70–6 and did it with the starters only playing one quarter in the second half of the two games.

In the final week of the season, Vickroy had to face Hamilton, whose only loss had gone to Central in their week 7 matchup. Hamilton had rebounded well from that blowout loss, and they were looking for some sort of redemption versus another great team in Vickroy. But this was a big game for Vickroy as well. This game would determine their seed in the state playoffs and would decide how early on they would face the presumptive number 1 seed, Central Catholic. If Vickroy won, they would most likely have the number 2 seed in the playoffs, which would mean they would only play Central if they both made it to the state championship game. But a loss would mean they would drop in seeding and most likely face Central much earlier in the playoffs. Vickroy knew they'd have to face Central at some point either way, but their goal was to go undefeated and not lose any momentum going into the playoffs.

In football, the most important games are played in the harshest weather conditions, and that's what makes the game unique. A lot of teams perform well in September when playing in ideal temperatures, with no rain or wind, but the teams that are special have the mental toughness to play just as well in frigid temperatures and snow on the ground. The toughest players enjoy this time in the season, but for many of the players, these late November and early December games are gruesome. Practices were cold, and it was starting to get dark early. This made it difficult for most teams to maintain the intensity throughout the week of practice, but not Vickroy. They had been looking forward to this opportunity ever since their loss to Central in last year's playoff game, and the enthusiasm on their team with the playoffs on the horizon was at its peak.

Hamilton Game

On the day of the Hamilton game, an article was published in which the Hamilton players were interviewed and asked about their upcoming matchup with Vickroy. Coach Thomas posted quotes from the article all over the Vickroy locker room to motivate the team. One quote said Jimmy was just a track star and wasn't capable of making plays in a physical battle. Another quote said that Sean was an overrated quarterback who couldn't make throws unless guys were wide open. When the team got into the locker room and saw those quotes posted on their lockers and all over the walls, they were infuriated. They were already a highly motivated team, and adding fuel to the fire was not a great idea for Hamilton.

When the game started, Coach Thomas made it a point to give Jimmy the ball on underneath routes so that he could get the team tough physical yards on the way to an early touchdown. He followed that up by spreading the field and letting Sean pick apart the Hamilton defense on the way to another first-quarter touchdown and a quick 14–0 lead. By the end of the first half, Vickroy was up 28–0, and Jimmy had two touchdowns and 130 all-purpose yards. The entire team was completely dialed in and all about business. They were making a statement, not only to Hamilton but to the entire state that they were one of the best teams in the country and should not be provoked. At halftime, Jimmy and the rest of the team convinced Coach Thomas to keep his foot on the gas and continue to make them pay for their comments in the news article. So Vickroy came right back out in the second half and put another fourteen points on the board before finally sitting the starters in the fourth quarter. They put a beating on Hamilton and didn't even let them sniff the red zone until the starters were taken out. The final score was 48–13. Vickroy finished the season undefeated and with all of their players healthy. It had been a long season, but the real season was just beginning. They had been looking forward to the playoffs all year, and anything less than a state title appearance would have been a disappointment to the fans, but the expectations inside of the Vickroy locker room were to win it all. Their chance had finally come.

First Round of Playoffs: Forest Hills High School

In the first round of the playoffs, Vickroy had to face Forest Hills, a team that went 6–4 and barely snuck into the playoffs. Although Forest Hills didn't have a great record, they played a very tough schedule and lost three of their games by less than a touchdown. They were a very physical team and could have easily won nine games if a couple of calls would have gone their way in those close games. Vickroy was well aware of what Forest Hills was capable of if they were overlooked. Coach Thomas always preached to play at a high level, no matter the opponent, and the players were mature enough to know that underestimating a team in the playoffs could lead to heartbreak.

Vickroy came out strong early in the game and got out to a 24–3 lead in the first half. By the end of the third quarter, they were able to take most of the starters out of the game and spent the fourth quarter just chewing the clock. Days dominated in the rushing attack and finished with over two hundred yards and four touchdowns on the ground. Jimmy, Sean, and EJ all added a touchdown of their own as they led Vickroy to a 49–17 victory in the first round.

Second Round of Playoffs: Clifton Hall High School

In the second round, Vickroy played the all-boys private school Clifton Hall. Clifton Hall was a lot like Central Catholic. They were known to recruit their athletes and had a lot of talent scattered throughout their roster. They went deep into the playoffs in the previous season but graduated a lot of starters and were in a bit of a rebuilding year. They had an 8–2 season, but they were very inconsistent all year. They had a Jekyll-and-Hyde team that would play perfect football for a half and then come out in the second half and turn the ball over every other possession. Vickroy didn't know which team they would have to face, but it didn't matter. Their job was to go out and execute their game plan to perfection and not worry about what the other team was doing.

Clifton Hall played tough in the first quarter, but after Vickroy got out to a ten-point lead midway through the second quarter, their confidence began to dwindle away, and they started making crucial mistakes. The score at halftime was 20–10 after Tim Hall got an interception to close out the second quarter. Vickroy received the ball to start the second half and scored another touchdown on their opening drive to make the score 27–10. Clifton Hall was unable to move the ball in the second half with Coach Thomas sending heavy pressure on every play. Linebacker Jeremy Rowley finished with eight sacks and seven tackles behind the line of scrimmage. Sean was the offensive player of the game accounting for all of Vickroy's six touchdowns, four rushing, and two passing, in the 42–10 win.

Semifinal Round of Playoffs: Pennwood High School

Vickroy was now one win away from taking a trip to Hershey to play in the state championship game. If Vickroy was able to get a win versus the undefeated Pennwood High Knights, they would most likely be facing Central Catholic in the title game, who had been dominating their playoff opponents. Vickroy could not afford to overlook Pennwood, who was having an impressive season of their own, but they were definitely paying attention to how well Central

Catholic was playing. Central Catholic's defense had been suffocating and had not given up a touchdown to anyone in the playoffs. They were expected to continue that dominance in their final playoff matchup versus Georgetown Prep.

Vickroy just needed to take care of business on their end, and they would get the revenge game that they had been hoping for. Pennwood was the number 3 ranked team in the state and were only a six-point underdog in the game versus Vickroy. They were a well-rounded team and didn't have any glaring weaknesses for Vickroy to expose. Vickroy was going to need to bring their A game to secure a win.

The game started off as a defensive struggle with the score being tied at 0–0 at the end of the first quarter. Pennwood was doing a good job of eliminating Vickroy's big passing plays, so Vickroy had to rely on the run game. In the second quarter, Vickroy was able to get the first touchdown of the game on a five-yard run by Ryan Days, after a long fifteen-play drive that consisted of eleven run plays. After getting another defensive stop, they put together another long and hard-fought drive to go up 14–0 going into the half.

In the third quarter, it was clear that Vickroy's running attack was really wearing down the Pennwood defense, and they were beginning to get fatigued. In addition to that, a potent running attack has a way of breaking a team's will, and that was beginning to happen to Pennwood. They knew what was coming, and they could not stop it. They were bruised, tired, and discouraged. Vickroy's offensive line was dominating, and Coach Thomas was content with letting them continue to open up running lanes for Days for the rest of the game.

By the end of the third quarter, Vickroy had gotten up to a 27–0 lead, and Pennwood was waving the white flag. They couldn't match Vickroy's physicality and had no shot at making a comeback. The final score was 37–0 as Vickroy dominated in a game that was expected to be much closer versus the number 3 team in the state. A shutout in this game gave Vickroy the confidence that they needed going into the title game. It was as an impressive victory of any in the state playoffs, and the guys were ready to take that momentum in to the big game.

The team celebrated their state championship berth, but there was one more game left to win. They weren't satisfied with just getting to the title game, their goal was to win it and anything less than that would have been a major disappointment. It was time to see everything they had worked for come to fruition, and the team was anxious to hoist that state championship trophy.

CHAPTER 6

❦

All in It

On the next Monday before practice started, Coach Thomas called a quick team meeting.

"Listen up, men. Before we get started, I gotta let you guys know that Ryan Days won't be here today. I don't have many details on the situation, and now wouldn't be the time to get into it if I did, but he got arrested over the weekend, and he won't be eligible to participate in the game this week. Now no matter what his situation is, we'll still consider him to be a part of this team, so we'll support him in any way that we can moving forward. But for now, the focus is Central Catholic. Next man up. We have playmakers on this team that can pick up the slack, and I expect you guys to step up. Justin has been chomping at the bit to get his opportunity to contribute, and here is his chance. We all know he's one of the best athletes on this team and brings speed and a dynamic style that I think will help us in a lot of ways. Days was obviously a huge part of this team, but this doesn't change anything. Our goal is still to win a championship on Saturday, and I still fully expect us to do that. We clear?"

"Yes, sir," they all said collectively.

"All right, let's go, men. Practice like champions."

Coach Thomas was confident in sophomore running back Justin Simmons, who hadn't seen any varsity action this year but had been dominating in the JV games, but the team was in shock. They were all concerned about what happened to their teammate and close friend. They were also concerned about losing one of their best players just before the title game. It was clearly bothering the team and affecting their ability to focus at practice, so Brandon asked Coach Thomas if he could pause practice for a moment to address the team.

"Bring it in," Brandon yelled after Coach Thomas blew his whistle.

"Everybody take your helmets off and take a knee. All eyes on me…A year ago, after losing to Central Catholic in the first round, we all came together and promised one another that we would sacrifice, work hard, and do everything in our power to win a championship this season. We hit the weights together as a team in a way that we never had before. Six-o'clock workouts on the field all summer—every day—for one purpose, one mission, one goal. A championship. I know we're all worried about Days, but I can tell you this, the last thing he would want is for us to come this far and lose this game because of a distraction that he caused. I know it's killing him that he can't play in this game with us, and it would hurt him even more if he felt like we didn't win it because of him. So instead of being down on ourselves, we're gonna get our heads straight, have a great week of practice, and go win this game."

The whole team stood to their feet and started to clap and get excited.

"Let's *go*! Let's *go*!" Brandon yelled as the team jumped up and down in a team circle.

"All right, fellas. Team on three, team on three. One, two, three!"

"Team!"

After Brandon's speech, the team returned to practice with a new focus. Everyone was still concerned about Ryan Days, but they knew that there was nothing they could do but to prepare themselves to win a championship. They practiced hard all week and approached every drill with the intensity and attention to detail that Coach Thomas wanted. The game plan was implemented, and the team was as prepared as they could be. Only thing that was left to do was to get out on the field and execute.

Travel Day

After a week of practice and school that felt like an eternity, the Friday before the long-awaited state championship game had finally come. Vickroy had been looking forward to getting a rematch with Central Catholic all season, and they were anxious to prove to everyone that they were the better team. Meanwhile Central Catholic was excited about the opportunity to return to the title game and come away with a victory this year. Both teams had a chip on their shoulders and wanted to prove that all of the hype was real. They both had been playing a level above everyone else in the state all season and were on a collision course that was shaping up to be one of the most competitive and anticipated state championship games of the decade.

The game would be played at Hershey Park Stadium on Saturday, and Friday was travel day. That morning, while Jimmy waited for Sean to pick him up, he and his mom had breakfast together. "What time is the bus leaving?" Deborah asked as she handed Jimmy his plate of egg whites, bacon, and toast.

"We're supposed to be leaving around nine. They want us to get there before noon so we can go to the stadium and do a walk-through before we check in to our hotel."

"Oh, okay. Well, hurry up and eat, it's already eight forty."

"Yeah, I know. Sean should be pulling up any second now."

"I put plenty of Gatorade and water in your bag. Make sure you hydrate. The last thing you need is to be cramping up out there tomorrow."

"Thanks, Mom. I'll make sure I drink fluids nonstop from now until game time. Nothing is gonna stop me from getting this win tomorrow."

"I know you'll be anxious, but make sure you stretch well too."

"Okay, Ma, I got it," Jimmy said as he heard Sean pull up and honk his horn.

"Okay, son, let me say a prayer with you before you go," Deborah said as Jimmy put his plate in the sink and started getting his bags together.

Deborah and Jimmy joined hands and bowed their heads.

"First and foremost, Father, we thank you for waking us this morning and giving us the opportunity to see another day. Thank you for your grace, your mercy, your love, your kindness, your forgiveness, your favor, your protection, and thank you for providing for us. We ask, Lord, that you blot out our sins and transgressions with the blood of Jesus Christ. Help us be obedient to your word and your will today. Help us to be a blessing unto others today. We ask, Father, for your protection as Jimmy travels today, and we ask that you protect him from injury on the field tomorrow. We ask for your favor in the game tomorrow, and if it is not in your will for us to get a win, we ask, Lord, that you help Jimmy to have the strength to handle a loss in the manner that you would like him to. We trust in you, and we give you thanks in advance. We love you, Lord. Amen."

"Amen. Thanks, Ma. I love you."

"I love you too, son. Good luck. I'll be watching on TV tomorrow," Deborah said as they hugged before Jimmy left.

When Jimmy and Sean got to the school parking lot, most of the team was already on the Greyhound bus. "Y'all made it just in time. We was about to leave y'all," Coach Thomas said jokingly.

"Yeah right, Coach," Jimmy said laughing.

"We not even late. It's eight fifty-eight," Sean said, smiling.

"If you ain't ten minutes early, you late. Y'all know that. Now get on the bus before we leave y'all here."

The guys laughed and got on the bus with their teammates. Coach Thomas was trying to keep things light as much as possible before the game. He knew that his team was ready, he just wanted them to play loose and do what they had been doing all year long. This was the first game all year that they were the underdogs, and he didn't want that pressure to get to them. Vickroy was already playing with a handicap with Days being ineligible for this game; he needed his team to be sharp and limit the mental mistakes in order to get a victory.

On the bus ride, the team watched movies, listened to music, slept, and went over the game plan with one another.

"Jeremy, we already know what they're gonna try to do on offense. They line up in a lot of different formations, but all they wanna do is get the ball to

Kevin Jones. Eighty percent of the time, they give up the play based on where he's lined up," Jimmy said.

"Right. If he's at running back, it's most likely a handoff, or they're throwing to him coming out of the backfield."

"Exactly," Tim Hall said.

As the guys went over their defensive scheme, Jimmy received a text from Samantha.

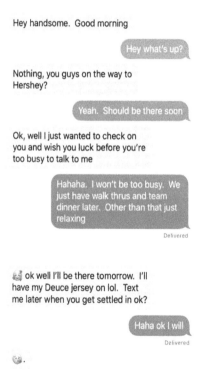

Jimmy was focused for this game, but he was really starting to like Samantha. He was happy that she would be there to see him play for a state title, and he was excited to put on a show for her on the biggest stage that he's played on so far. He tried not to think about it too much, but he was looking forward to getting to spend more time with her after the season was over.

As the bus arrived at the Hershey facilities, Coach Thomas stood up to address the team.

"All right, men, we're almost there. When we get there, we'll go out on the field and do walk-throughs. We'll go offense first and then defense, then we'll go over special teams. When you get off the bus, I don't wanna hear any laughing and joking. We're here for business, so let's be about our business. Lock in and focus. It's time to go to work."

"Yes, sir."

When the team got off the bus, everyone immediately began to concentrate on the task at hand. The allure of just being at Hershey Stadium made the reality that they were finally at the state championship game set in. In the previous year, they were eliminated from the playoffs early and had to watch Central Catholic play in the state championship game on TV. This year everyone in the state would be watching them, and they were prepared for this moment.

During the walk-through, everyone was sharp. They approached it with the right intensity, and they didn't have any mental errors. They spent all off season working to be physically and mentally prepared, and Coach Thomas knew he had done everything he could do to have them ready for this moment. All that was left to do was to get out on the field and execute. But no matter the outcome, Coach Thomas was confident they had done everything in their power to give themselves a shot to win this game.

After the walk-through, the team got checked in to the hotel, which was a mile away from the stadium on the Hershey Park grounds. They had a few hours of downtime to just relax before team dinner at the hotel, so the guys just hung out in their rooms and played video games. Everyone was anxious to get to Saturday, so they were just trying to kill time to get the day over with. While Jimmy watched some of the guys play Madden, he got a text from Samantha.

When it was time for dinner, the team met in the main lobby of the hotel. Coach Thomas did roll call to make sure everyone was there, and then they went into the hotel ballroom for a buffet-style dinner. The hotel served baked ziti, chicken breast, salad, and dinner rolls. "Make sure y'all are getting your carbs and hydrate. Fuel the machine," Coach Thomas said to everyone as they made their plates. The players all sat down and ate. The mood was light as everyone laughed and joked while they ate. This was an experience that they had been looking forward to all of their lives, and although it was a business trip, Coach Thomas was happy to see the guys relaxed and enjoying themselves. After everyone finished eating, it was time for the team to have final meetings in the hotel conference room before the big game.

During the meeting, the coaching staff went over the offensive and defensive game plans and answered any final questions the team had about the scheme. The meeting was short, but it was the coaches' final opportunity to make sure the team was mentally prepared for the task at hand.

After the meetings were over, most of the players went back to their rooms to play more video games, but Jimmy got his playbook and took a walk out to the stadium. When he got to the stadium, the field lights were on, the stands were empty, and everything was quiet, but he could still sense an enormous energy in the air. He walked up and down the field, envisioning himself defending the plays that he anticipated seeing from Central and scoring touchdowns on offense. In less than twenty-four hours, Jimmy hoped to be celebrating a state championship victory with his teammates. It was so close he could taste it. He was completely focused and ready to make it happen. After about an hour, he went back to his hotel room and tried to get some rest, but he was so anxious that he could barely sleep. After lying in bed for an hour, he eventually dozed off and was off to dreaming about the big game the next day.

The next afternoon, the team had brunch together at the hotel and then got on the bus to go to the stadium. On the short bus ride to the stadium, everyone was quiet and focused. As they got off of the bus and walked into the locker room, most of the guys had their headphones on, listening to music. There was no more talking, laughing, and joking. They all had one thing on their minds—victory.

While everyone was in the locker room getting geared up, Jimmy went into the athletic trainer's room to get stretched and taped up. This was a normal practice for Jimmy before each game, but today the mood was different. Even the athletic trainers were paying more attention to detail in their tasks for this game. They didn't get the same recognition as the players or coaches, but they were a part of the team as well, and they were just as excited for a state title as anyone.

Once Jimmy was done getting his ankles and wrists taped by the training staff, he went back into the locker room to put his uniform on and say a quick prayer before it was time to head out to the field.

He took a knee at the foot of his locker and began to pray. "Lord, thank you for helping us to get here. We've worked so hard. Please help us to stay injury-free and play well. Please give us your favor and grant us with a victory. In Jesus's name. Amen."

"It's almost game time, men!" Coach Thomas yelled as he walked in the locker room. "You got butterflies? That's good. But don't be nervous, be anxious to go out there and prove that you're the best team in this state. Let's go. We heading out in fifteen minutes."

Once everyone was dressed and ready to go, Coach Thomas came back into the locker room.

"All right, men it's go time, listen up, listen up. Bring it in close," Coach Thomas said as he walked to the center of the locker room, and everyone gathered around him. "What we've accomplished so far this year has been special. Undefeated, five shutouts, and a forty-point-per-game average. But none of it means anything if we don't finish it. Everything we've worked for, sacrificed for, and prayed for is here for the taking. Just because we've worked hard doesn't mean they're gonna give it to us, we gotta take it. They worked hard too. Respect isn't earned by the hard work you put in during the off season, it's taken out there on the field. They've been questioning the hype all year, well, it's time to go out there and show 'em what it's all about. Take what's yours! Jimmy, break us down!"

"All right, fellas, no more talking, no more speculating, now we gonna let our pads speak. I want victory on three. One, two, three."

"Victory!" the whole team screamed and ran out of the locker room, led by Coach Thomas.

When they got out to the field, the stadium was packed, and the energy was high. The temperature was in the high forties, and there was no precipitation. It was perfect weather for a game in December.

"Captains, captains," Coach Thomas yelled to tell the team captains to let them know that it was time to go out to midfield for the coin toss.

As the captains walked out to midfield, Coach Thomas paced the sideline talking to the team. "This is what we've all been waiting for. All the blood, sweat, and tears for this moment. For this opportunity. This is your time, men."

When the captains got to midfield, the referee began going over the rules of the coin toss. "Okay, gentlemen, congratulations on making it to the Pennsylvania Class 4A state championship game. You've both had remarkable undefeated seasons, but there can be only one champion, and today will decide that. Good luck out there. Central Catholic, you're the home team, so you get to call the coin toss," he said, showing both groups of team captains the coin. "This side with the state of Pennsylvania is heads, and this side with the football on it is tails. Got it?"

"Yes, sir," Kevin Jones said.

"Okay, call it in the air," he said as he flipped the coin.

"Heads."

"The call is heads. Okay, it is a heads. Central Catholic, do you want to receive or defer to the second half?"

"We'll defer."

"Vickroy, Central Catholic is choosing to defer to the second half, do you want to kick or receive?"

"We'll receive it going this way," Jimmy said as he pointed to return the ball with the wind at their backs.

"All right, Central Catholic has won the toss. They've elected to defer to the second half. Vickroy will receive the ball."

"Return team, return team," Coach Thomas yelled to tell the kickoff return team to get ready.

As the team captains walked back to the sideline, the team ran out to meet them on the field.

"*Woo-hoo! It's showtime! It's showtime!* Let's fly around, boys. Every play one hundred miles per hour. Give it all you got! Kick return team, let's start it off right with a big return," Jeremy yelled as the team gathered around him.

When Jimmy went back to receive the kick, he looked to the stands and spotted Samantha. When they made eye contact, he patted his chest and pointed to her to acknowledge that he saw her. Then he took a deep breath and got set to return the kick. His heart was pounding, but he was ready.

Central kicked the ball deep right to Jimmy. They weren't going to show Vickroy the respect of trying to kick away from him like many of the other teams. The players were arrogant, and so were the coaches. They wanted to send a message on the first kickoff that they weren't intimidated by anyone on Vickroy's team.

Jimmy caught the ball in the back of the end zone for a touchback, and Vickroy started the opening drive on the twenty-yard line. Sean got in the huddle and gave the play call.

"Let's start this thing off right. Gun slot right, 98 X wheel, halfback check. On two, on two, Ready."

"Break."

The offense came to the line of scrimmage in a shotgun formation, with Jimmy lined up at the slot receiver position. Sean surveilled the defense and saw the linebackers creeping toward the line of scrimmage, preparing to blitz. With the linebackers blitzing, Sean knew he would need more time to get the throw off, so he called an audible.

"Lucky Max, lucky Max. Set, hike! Hike!"

When the ball snapped, the linebackers blitzed off of the edge, just as Sean expected, Justin Simmons made a great block and gave Sean time to roll out of the pocket to his right. Once Sean escaped the pocket, he looked up and saw Jimmy running open down the sideline on the wheel route. With a defender in pursuit, Sean threw the ball as far as he could and hit Jimmy in perfect stride. Jimmy caught the ball and coasted to the end zone on the very first offensive play of the game. The Vickroy sideline exploded, and the crowd roared. Vickroy knew they would have to put up points to beat Central Catholic, and the night could not have gotten off to a better start.

"Gonna be a *long* night!" Jimmy said to some of the Central Catholic players as he tossed the ball to the referee and celebrated with his teammates.

Vickroy was confident that they were the better team, but Central Catholic was not a team that they could agitate without consequence.

On the ensuing kickoff, Vickroy did not want to make the mistake of allowing Kevin Jones to swing the momentum back in the favor of Central Catholic with a big kick return, so they squib-kicked the kickoff, and Central started their drive at the forty-yard line.

On Central's first play, they lined up in a spread formation with Kevin Jones split out at wide receiver, and Adam Sanchez ran a quarterback draw. He was able to pick up fifteen yards on the play. On the next play, Jones lined up in the backfield, and they were able to pick up another first down on a halfback screen. Just like that, Central was on the Vickroy twenty-yard line looking to punch it in the end zone and tie the game up at seven points.

On the next play, Central lined up in an empty formation. Based on film study, Vickroy knew that when they lined up in this formation, they were looking to take a shot deep. Jimmy focused his attention to Kevin Jones who was lined up at the slot position. At the snap, Jones took off deep, straight down the middle of the field. Sanchez tried to look off the safeties by focusing on the outside receivers, but Jimmy knew where the ball was going. When Jones got about twelve yards downfield, Sanchez threw it to him, leading him deep into the back of the end zone. As the ball came down, Jimmy had perfect coverage on Jones. They both jumped dove to make a play on the ball, and with Jimmy draped all over him, Jones reached out with one hand and pulled the ball in while dragging his foot in the back of the end zone. It was a remarkable play, and what made it even more significant was that he made the play over Jimmy.

The fact that Central drove the ball down the field so easily had Vickroy concerned and seeing Jimmy get beat for the first time was even more of a morale killer.

When Vickroy got the ball, they weren't able to get anything going. They tried to run, but Central Catholic's Boomer Hicks was all over it. They tried to pass, but the coverage was tight, and the pass rush forced Sean to get rid of the ball quickly. They went three and out and had to punt the ball back to Central with the score tied at 7–7.

Central started their next drive on their own thirty with all the momentum in their favor, and their confidence was soaring.

Sanchez then began to lead his team down the field on a drive that was more impressive than the first, carving the Vickroy defense up for sixty yards on four straight pass completions. After a short run by Jones, Central was just inside the ten-yard line with a first and goal.

On the next play, they came out in an I formation. Sanchez snapped the ball, faked the handoff to Kevin Jones, and rolled out to his right on a bootleg. Sanchez looked to throw the ball to the tight end who was running a crossing route across the field, but it was covered by the Vickroy defense, so he tucked the ball and started running toward the end zone. When Jeremy saw that Sanchez was running it in, he left the man that he was covering and began to pursue the quarterback. When Sanchez got to the three-yard line, just before Jeremy could make the tackle, he dove for the pylon for the touchdown just as the first quarter ended.

Central was up 14–7, and Vickroy desperately needed to answer with a score of their own to prevent the game from getting out of hand.

After another touchback on the kickoff, Vickroy started their next drive on the twenty-yard line. Coach Thomas decided to go with the running attack to try to drain the clock and keep the ball out of the hands of the Central offense that was on fire. Vickroy was able to get a few first downs running the football, but without Days in the backfield, the drive eventually stalled at about the Central Catholic forty-yard line.

Vickroy was able to burn a lot of clock, but they found themselves having to punt again with about three minutes left in the first half. Vickroy had a great punt out of bounds and pinned Central Catholic inside their own twenty-yard line.

When Central Catholic got back on offense, they had no intentions of being conservative and running the clock out. They were up by a touchdown, but a score here, right before the half, would be a backbreaker for Vickroy. On the first play of the drive, they came out firing. Sanchez dropped back and took a shot deep and connected with a wide receiver on the sideline for a twenty-five-yard gain. On the next play, they ran a draw, and Kevin Jones ripped off a solid sixteen-yard gain. On the next two plays, Central tried play action passes, but Vickroy covered it well and forced an incompletion on both attempts.

Central was now looking at a third and long with under a minute left on the game clock. They came out of the huddle and lined up in an empty formation. Jimmy focused on Kevin Jones who was lined up at slot receiver. On the snap, all of the receivers ran vertical routes, but the Vickroy defense had it covered well. Sanchez looked downfield and saw Jimmy covering Jones, but instead of taking another shot, he tucked the ball and took off up the middle of the field. He made Jeremy miss with a nifty move and ran for a thirty-five-yard pickup before being brought down by Tim Hall at the Vickroy thirty-five-yard line.

With about twenty-three seconds left on the game clock, Central quickly lined up and ran a halfback screen to Jones where he was able to follow his blocks to get a twenty-yard gain and get out of bounds at the Vickroy fifteen-yard line to stop the clock with eight seconds left in the half.

Vickroy's defense was gassed and starting to panic as Central seemed to be moving the ball down the field with such ease. Central's coach knew Vickroy's defense was beginning to feel overwhelmed, so he stuck with the aggressive play calls instead of playing it safe for the field goal.

On the next play, Central came out in an empty formation again. This time, Vickroy knew to be aware of Sanchez's running ability. On the snap, Central ran all vertical routes, and Vickroy played a zone coverage to take away the threat of a Sanchez scramble, but instead of running it, Sanchez threw it to a receiver underneath of the deep zone coverage. The Central Catholic receiver caught the ball at about the ten-yard line, broke a tackle immediately, and bulldozed another Vickroy defender over as he crossed the goal line for a touchdown as time expired in the first half.

As the teams went into the locker rooms for halftime, the spirits of the two sides couldn't have been more opposite. Central was riding a high after getting a late touchdown to take the 21–7 lead, and Vickroy was in shock going into halftime facing a deficit for the first time all year.

When Vickroy got into the locker room, everyone was quiet. Most of the players were starting to question if they were good enough to beat this Central team. When Coach Thomas got into the locker room, he could clearly see that his team was discouraged. "Heads up, men, we're still in this game. We took their best shot. Now let's recover and return some shots of our own," he said while starting to draw up the game plan adjustments on the dry-erase board.

"Jimmy, talk to me, man. What do we gotta do out there?" Sean asked Jimmy.

"We just gotta keep fighting, man. We're still in this game. I gave up a touchdown on that first drive and haven't been able to get anything going offensively. I'll make it up to you guys in the second half, I promise. Just keep fighting, bro."

Jimmy was disappointed in his performance in the first half, but his confidence was still high. He knew that they were just a few big plays away from being right back in the game, and he believed that he would be the one to make those plays for his team in the second half.

After the halftime adjustments were in, Jimmy stood up to address the team.

"Look, guys, I know that first half didn't go the way we wanted it to, we gave up big plays and left plays out there on the field. But the first half is over with. Let's put it behind us. When we go out there in the second half, it's zero to zero. Take it one play at a time and execute. Just focus on beating your man, doing your job on *this* play. Don't look up at the scoreboard until the game clock is at zero. Don't be intimidated, don't be discouraged, just go out there and have fun. We all love playing this game, so just enjoy it out there. The big plays will come if we just have fun and believe in one another." He looked everyone in the eye intensely. "Believe, men. Believe. Bring it in and let's break it down. Believe on three, believe on three. One, two, three."

"Believe!"

As they ran back out to the field, Coach Thomas hit Jimmy on the shoulder pads. "Show 'em who the best player in the state is," he said.

"Yes, sir."

Vickroy had to kick off to start the second half. Central Catholic was looking to put the game away on the first drive of the second half with another touchdown. A three-touchdown lead would have most likely been a knockout blow.

Central started with the ball on their forty-yard line after another squib kick by Vickroy. On their first two plays, they seemed to pick right back up where they left off in the first half by gashing the Vickroy defense on two big gains.

They were in Vickroy territory quickly, and they were not slowing down the tempo. On first and ten on the Vickroy thirty-yard line, Central lined up in a shotgun spread formation with Kevin Jones in the backfield. Sanchez snapped the ball and threw it to Jones on the checkdown. Jones caught the ball with a lot of room to work and started sprinting through the middle of the Vickroy defense. Tim Hall came in to make the tackle, but Jones hurdled him in stride. His athleticism was amazing, and it was on full display; but as Jones came down, Jimmy came out of nowhere, punched the ball and jarred it loose. Jeremy dove on it and recovered the fumble on the Vickroy fifteen-yard line. It was the big play that Vickroy desperately needed to get back in the game, and Jimmy delivered it.

The Vickroy offense got back on the field and huddled up.

"Here we go. One play at a time. Let's execute. I right 22 gator on 1, I right 22 gator on 1. Ready."

"Break."

On the first play of the drive, Vickroy lined up in an I formation and ran a quick pass to Jimmy. He caught the ball, made his man miss, made a quick cut back inside that made two defenders fall, and ran for forty yards before being brought down at the fifty-yard line.

"I'm activated! Let's go!" Jimmy said as they got back into the huddle.

On the next play, they went right back to Jimmy, completing a twenty-yard pass on a corner route to the sideline. Vickroy had Central on their heels with their fast-paced offense. On the next three plays, Vickroy handed the ball to Justin Simmons who was able to gain another first down on three straight four-yard carries.

Vickroy now had first and ten from the Central twenty-yard line.

"All right, let's go empty, motion Z option, smash Y go on 2, empty, motion Z option, smash Y go on 2. Ready."

"Break."

Vickroy came to the line of scrimmage, and Sean surveilled the defense. As EJ went in motion, Sean saw Boomer, the Central linebacker, following him across the formation, indicating man-to-man coverage. When the ball was snapped, EJ ran straight up the hash, put a double move on the linebacker, and flew by him. Sean knew that none of Central's defenders could cover EJ in man-to-man coverage, so as soon EJ looked back for the ball, Sean hit him with a strike. EJ caught the pass and easily sprinted to the end zone to make it a one-score game. It was revenge for EJ, and the whole team was fired up to see him make Boomer look silly on a big play in the state championship game.

On Central and Vickroy's next possessions, they exchanged touchdowns to make the score 21–28 going into the fourth quarter.

At the start of the final quarter, Vickroy had the ball and needed a touchdown to tie the game. The Central defense could not stop the Vickroy offense in the third quarter, and for Vickroy to have a shot at coming back and winning the game, they could not afford to be stopped in the fourth either. Central did a good job of limiting the big plays from Vickroy, but the offense was still able to methodically march the ball down the field and get into the end zone, capping the drive off with a touchdown by Jimmy on a slant route. The game was now tied at 28–28, and the Vickroy offense looked unstoppable, but it was up to the Vickroy defense—which had been struggling all evening—to get a stop.

Everyone in the stadium knew that this was a crucial drive in the game, and that meant that Vickroy was going to get a heavy dose of Kevin Jones. On the first four plays, they got the ball in the hands of their best player, and he was able to pick up two first downs. On the next play, Sanchez hit a receiver on a fade route on the sideline for a twenty-yard gain. Central was in Vickroy territory once again and looking to take the lead again about midway through the final quarter. After giving Jones a short break, Central went right back to him on the next two plays, but he was only able to pick up four yards. On third and six, Central ran a screen pass to Jones, which they had success on early in the game, but Jeremy read it perfectly and was able to make a tackle for a short gain.

On fourth down, Central lined up for a thirty-five-yard field goal, and their all-state kicker connected to take a three-point lead.

Vickroy got the ball back with four minutes left in the game. They needed at least a field goal to tie the game and send it to overtime or a touchdown to win. They needed to be aggressive enough to get points, but they could not afford a turnover this late in the game.

They started the drive on their twenty-yard line after the touchback.

"All right, guys, this is it. One more drive. No matter what, we played our hearts out tonight, and I'm proud of you guys. But let's put it together one more time and get this win. I need everything you got. Leave it all on the field, and we'll be champions.

They haven't stopped us all half and they're nervous. Their sideline is quiet. Let's take it to 'em!" Sean said in the huddle.

Vickroy came out in a shotgun formation, and Sean was operating the offense with decisive and accurate precision passes. The way he was spreading the ball around to different receivers and reading the defensive coverages was too much for Central to handle. He was in a zone like he had never been before, and the Central sideline knew they were in trouble.

Vickroy ran about two minutes off the clock, taking the ball down to the Central Catholic thirty-eight-yard line. They were getting close to the range of their kicker and needed at least ten more yards for a realistic field goal try, but they had their eyes set on scoring a touchdown and putting the game away.

On the next play, Sean dropped back to pass and didn't find any open receivers, but he was able to scramble for a ten-yard gain. With Vickroy now in reasonable field goal range, Central was expecting to see more conservative play calls, but they were wrong. Vickroy was going for the win.

Sean took a knee in the center of the huddle and looked his teammates in their eyes. "Bring it in, guys. We're not leaving this game in the hands of a field goal. We're getting in the end zone. They can't stop us. Gun right, 99 choice on two, gun right 99 choice on two. Ready."

"Break!"

The offense came to the line of scrimmage in a shotgun formation with four wide receivers. As soon as the ball was snapped, the Central linebackers blitzed off the edges. Sean had to get the ball out of his hands quickly, so he checked it down Justin Simmons in the flats who picked up a short four-yard gain. The Central defense was able to make the tackle in bounds and kept the clock rolling. Vickroy was still in good position with a second and six on the Central twenty-four-yard line, but now the clock was becoming a concern, so Vickroy took a time-out.

During the time-out, the Vickroy offense went to the sideline to discuss the next play with Coach Thomas.

"Hey, hey, we're good. We're right where we want to be. We're gonna punch it in right here. This game is ours. We're goin' Ace Jet. I need everyone to dial in, make your block, but do not get a penalty on a hold or block in the back. Everything we worked for will be decided in the next few plays. Champions on three. One, two, three."

"Champions!"

Vickroy came out of the time-out and went straight to the line of scrimmage. Sean lined up under the center and gave Jimmy the cue to go in motion. As Jimmy motioned across, the defense shifted to the side that he was motioning to. When Jimmy got close, Sean snapped the ball and handed it directly to him. As soon as Jimmy got the ball, the Central defensive end dove in for the tackle, but Jimmy avoided him with a quick move. As Jimmy bounced it to the outside, the Central cornerback was able to shed EJ's block. When he went in to tackle Jimmy low, Jimmy hurdled him. Jimmy raced down the sideline with only two defenders to beat. He made a quick jump cut to make the first one miss, then bounced off another tackle with a spin move back inside, and dove into the end zone for the touchdown.

The Vickroy crowd went wild as the band played the Vickroy fight song, and the team celebrated in the end zone. Vickroy had taken a 35–31 lead with fifteen seconds left on the clock. The sensational play by Jimmy was the exclamation point that he was looking for. He was dominant all year, and this performance in the state championship game, with all eyes on him, was the icing on the cake.

It was pandemonium on the Vickroy sideline, but there was still a little bit of time left on the clock, and Coach Thomas needed to get everyone to calm down and focus to prevent a catastrophic letdown.

"Settle down, settle down. Kickoff team, listen up. Squib kick again. Do not kick it out of bounds. We can't give them good enough field position for a Hail Mary. Jimmy, play the safety and make the tackle if anything breaks, got it?"

"Yes, sir."

The kickoff team got set and squib-kicked the ball on the kickoff. The ball took a hard bounce, and Kevin Jones was able to pick it up in stride at the thirty-yard line. He tried to run the ball to the left, but there was a wall of Vickroy defenders, so he reversed field and took it to the right where he had a host of blockers. Jones had some daylight, but there were still Vickroy defenders that had the angle on him.

When the first one tried to bring him down, Jones gave him a devastating stiff arm. Another defender had a shot at him, but Jones outran his pursuit angle. A nightmare was taking place right before Vickroy's eyes as Jones ran full speed down the sideline with one person to beat—Jimmy.

Kevin Jones was fast, but not fast enough to outrun Jimmy. As Jimmy got closer, Jones tried to cut back inside, but Jimmy adjusted well and dove in for the tackle. Jimmy had him around the waist, but Jones shook him off and broke from his grasp. Jimmy hit the turf as he watched Jones showboat on his way to the end zone with the time expired and no flags on the field. The entire Central Catholic sideline ran onto the field as they celebrated another state championship victory. Jimmy could not believe he let Jones get away from him. As he sat there on the field, just watching Central celebrate, he wanted to just crawl in a hole and disappear.

The whole game had been a roller coaster of emotions, and for it to end in that way had the Vickroy sideline in disbelief. They were in shock, and Coach Thomas didn't have many words for the team afterward. He was proud of his team, but he knew there weren't any words that could console them after such a heartbreaking defeat. They shook hands with the Central Catholic players who now had a new respect for Vickroy after a tough game that went down to the wire. Then they went into the locker room to change and got on the bus to go back to New Crofton.

CHAPTER 7

The Blame Game

After the loss, the team was devastated. They worked so hard and thought they had done enough to win the game in the final minutes but let it slip away on the final kickoff. Losing in that way made it much more difficult to accept. After last year's loss in the playoffs, they were definitely upset, but the expectations for this season were much higher, and to say they were disappointed would be an understatement. On the long bus ride home back to New Crofton, there wasn't a peep from any of them. Even Coach Thomas, who usually finds the silver lining in any circumstance, was noticeably shaken after the loss. He knew that his team put in the hard work and prepared properly. He preached all year that if they trained hard, practiced hard, and played hard on game day that they would be rewarded with a state championship; but unfortunately it did not work out that way. Coach Thomas had won and lost a state championship when he was in high school, so he knew how it felt to be on both sides. He really wanted his team to experience the thrill of being on the winning side after an early exit in the playoffs the previous season.

When the bus arrived back at Vickroy, many of the parents waited in the parking lot. They were there to support their boys after a tough loss. Before they got off of the bus, Coach Thomas addressed the team.

"All right, men, I know we're all hurting and disappointed but keep your heads held high. We came up short of our ultimate goal, but we played hard, and we have the respect of everyone we played against. Your parents and I are proud of all you guys. When you get off this bus, I don't wanna see anyone pouting, copy?"

"Yes, sir," the team said collectively.

"All right, see y'all in the morning at nine o'clock to turn in equipment."

When Jimmy got off the bus, he saw his mom, Deborah, standing by her car, wearing a Vickroy High hoodie with his number on it. She knew that Jimmy was taking the loss hard and just wanted to console and comfort him. He walked over to her and gave her a big hug.

"Hey, baby, how you doing?" she said in a soft and concerned tone.

"I'm okay, Ma, just sucks because I know we're better than those guys, and I felt like we deserved it," Jimmy replied as they got in the car to drive home.

"Yeah, I know you've been working so hard. We'll get 'em next year."

"I don't know. Next year will be a whole new team. You just never know. This was our year, and we let it slip away. I let it slip away," Jimmy said, shaking his head.

Jimmy blamed himself for the loss after missing the tackle on the final kickoff. Although he had done so much to get them there, he felt like he let his team and everyone at Vickroy down. The loss in the previous season was heartbreaking, but Jimmy felt a lot more personal responsibility for this one, and it was going to take him a while to bounce back from the disappointment.

The mood at school in the week following the championship loss was somber. The faculty, staff, and entire student body were experiencing a hangover after the emotional roller coaster in the championship game that ended in dismay. It had been a long season, not only for the players but for everyone at Vickroy, and the entire school was exhausted. They cheered for and supported the team all season with an expectation of winning a title, and when that didn't happen, it was deflating to the school spirit at Vickroy.

Jimmy ran indoor track at Vickroy during the winter, and since they went to the state championship game, the football season extended into the beginning of track season. Although his body was a little beat up after the long and physical football season, Jimmy went to track practice mainly to stretch and work on technique. He tried to give himself a few weeks to get into the proper condition before competing in any meets, but it was good for him to join the track team immediately after the conclusion of the football season in order to be best prepared as soon as possible.

Jimmy had been pretty distant from everyone, including Samantha and his closest friends, all week, but on that Wednesday after track practice, Jimmy received a text from Sean.

> I know you're still hurting over the game but come with me to the G Bar later. We need to get out and shake off this funk

> Yeah that's cool bro. What time?

> I'll come pick you up after I leave basketball practice. So around 6:30/6:45

> Ok cool

Jimmy walked home after track practice and got showered and changed. While he sat on the couch, waiting for Sean to pick him up, his mom, Deborah, came in from work.

"Hey, Ma."

"Hey, Jim, how you feeling?"

"I'm okay."

"You hungry? I'm gonna cook some chili."

"Sean is on his way over. We're gonna go get wings. If that's cool."

"Okay, that's fine. I heard that it might snow later, so if it does, make sure you're back before it gets bad."

"Okay. I see him pulling up now," Jimmy said as he grabbed his coat from the coatrack.

"Okay, have fun. Love you."

"Thanks Ma. Love you."

When Jimmy and Sean got to the G Bar, they sat a table in front of a big-screen television and started watching the NBA game that was on. They ordered drinks and wings and sat and talked while they waited for their food.

"So Days got arrested for fighting again, huh?" Sean asked.

"Yeah, he broke some dude's jaw. But I heard he didn't start it."

"He usually doesn't. But he's always the one to finish it."

"Yeah, I know. He can't control his temper," Jimmy said, shaking his head.

"He's a good guy, man. He just always seems to be in the wrong place at the wrong time."

"I hope he doesn't have to go to juvie for that."

"Yeah, me too. Did you hear that Tim Hall got offered to play at Columbia?" Sean asked.

"Yeah, he told me yesterday in English class. I'm happy for him."

"Yeah, man, he's pumped…I know this is a touchy subject, but did you hear that Kevin Jones got offers from Clemson, LSU, and Ohio State on Monday?"

"Yup, heard that too," Jimmy said as he let out a sigh.

"You get any calls this week."

"Nope."

"You will, bro. Don't trip."

"Wherever I go, I'm gonna go off, and every school that doesn't offer me is gonna regret it."

"My man, that's what I like to hear. Look, our wings are coming."

A lot of high school players in the area were getting scholarship offers from schools all over the country, and although Jimmy already had quite a few offers, he hadn't gotten an offer from any of the big colleges that he hoped to hear from. He was disappointed in the championship loss, but it was even more hurtful to see other guys getting scholarship offers from the schools that he dreamed of attending. He wasn't able to lead his school to a state championship, and the big schools were unsure if he had what it took to be productive at the next level. The lack of offers motivated him even more, but nonetheless, it was painful because he felt disrespected and unappreciated. He felt like he had just as good of a season as anyone in the state, but schools weren't completely sold on him because he came up short in the big game. Jimmy and Sean ate their wings and had some laughs, but Jimmy was fuming on the inside and was determined to make anyone who doubted him into a believer.

"I didn't even realize the snow started, it's coming down pretty hard out there," Jimmy said as he looked out the window.

"Yeah, hopefully we get off of school tomorrow." Sean laughed.

"I doubt it will get that bad. But if it does, I'm cool with that."

"You never know. Hey, can we get the check please?" Sean asked the waitress.

"Out of the offers that you have so far, where do you think you wanna go?" Jimmy asked.

"Man, I'm not sure. I think I would go to that FCS school Duquesne, in Pittsburgh," Sean said.

"Yeah, I heard that's a great school. They play some good ball out there too. I might go there with you, bro."

"Nah, man, you'll get that big offer. It's coming. What other schools are you thinking about?"

"I don't know because I haven't given it much thought. I got offers from Maryland, Rutgers, Temple, Syracuse, Duke, and a few others, but I been waiting to get an offer from a big school like Alabama, LSU, or Clemson. Which I know I would have gotten if we had won that game."

"Don't sweat it, man. You could get that call tonight or tomorrow. Just stay positive."

"Yeah, you're right. Let's get out of here, man. The snow looks like it's starting to stick out there."

"Yeah, let's roll."

The guys paid their bills and got in the car to leave the G Bar. Jimmy was feeling a little better about everything after getting out and hanging with Sean for a few hours. On the way to Jimmy's house, the guys listened to music and talked about basketball and track.

"Yo, when is the first basketball game?" Jimmy asked.

"It's on Friday, bro. You better be there to support your boy."

"Of course I'll be there." Jimmy laughed.

"You better. This snow is coming down pretty hard. I can barely see, man."

"Turn on the defrost and take it slow."

"I don't have no defrost." Sean laughed.

"Ah, man," Jimmy said as he shook his head with his hand on his forehead.

"Bro, I got this."

"You got it in four-wheel drive?"

"Yeah, man, and I just got new snow tires. We're not even sliding at all, relax."

"All right, man, just asking."

"Nah, just passenger-side driving is what you doing."

"Whatever, man." Jimmy laughed.

"How are things with Samantha?" Sean asked.

"Haven't heard from her."

"Really? What's up with that?"

"I don't know, bro. I don't really care to be honest."

"Man, I thought y'all were official."

"Nah, but it's all good. Gives me less distractions, you know?"

"Damn, bro. But honestly, I can't say I'm disappointed. Happy to have my wingman back. It hurt to see you all wifed up," Sean said, laughing as he nudged Jimmy's elbow.

"When is the first track meet that you're running in?" Sean asked.

"Next Friday. Gotta give myself a week to—"

Jimmy looked to his right and saw headlights from another car coming straight toward him. As the driver laid on the horn, the car slid toward them at full speed and *boom*!

The car crashed into Sean's car, making direct impact on the passenger side where Jimmy sat, and sent them off into a ditch on the side of the road. The passenger side window was completely shattered, and the door and front fender were smashed in. Both Jimmy and Sean were unconscious. As Sean started to regain consciousness, he tried to unbuckle his seat belt but was unable to.

"Jim, Jim. You all right, bro?" Sean said, half-conscious, with his voice trembling, but Jimmy didn't respond.

"Jim, wake up, bro. I think I dislocated my shoulder," he said in pain as he started to cry.

"Are you kids okay?" the man from the other car yelled as he approached their car.

"Call 911, we can't get out." Sean cried out.

"I already did. Help is on the way. I'm so sorry, I slid on the ice. Just hang on, guys."

As they waited for an ambulance, Sean continued to try to wake Jimmy, but he was unresponsive. The entire passenger side of the car was destroyed, there was blood on the airbag, and the inside of the doorframe. Jimmy's seat was pushed onto the top of the center console of the car. If Jimmy was alive, he appeared to be severely injured.

When the ambulance arrived, they were able to get Sean out of the vehicle pretty quickly, but because the damage to the passenger side of the car was so extensive, they had to get the Jaws of Life to remove Jimmy. Sean was able to walk on his own and didn't seem to have any life-threatening injuries, but his right arm was in a lot of pain. As they removed Jimmy from the vehicle, they put him on a stretcher and evaluated him for signs of life.

"He has a pulse and appears to be breathing!" the paramedic yelled.

As they put Jimmy into the ambulance, Jimmy started to groan in pain. Once inside the ambulance, the paramedics immediately started to cut away all of Jimmy's clothing to further evaluate the extent of his injuries. Jimmy's right leg was mangled and bloody, and he also had a large gash on his forehead and face. As the ambulance raced to the hospital, the paramedic administered oxygen to Jimmy and kept encouraging him to hang on.

When they arrived at the emergency room, they immediately took Jimmy in for X-rays and further evaluation. Sean was treated for a dislocated shoulder and diagnosed with a concussion. They released him, but he stuck around to hear the status of Jimmy's condition. Jimmy's mom, Deborah, arrived shortly after, and the hospital staff informed her of what happened. They explained to her that he was in stable condition and was being evaluated for injuries. Both Deborah and Sean anxiously waited in the waiting room to hear the results of the evaluation. After waiting for about an hour that felt more like ten hours, the doctor and surgeon came out to talk with Deborah.

"Ms. Lawson, your son is doing okay. He does not have any life-threatening injuries, but the injuries to his right side are severe. He's suffered a dislocated hip, compound fractures in his femur, fibula, and tibia, as well as ligament damage in his knee. He also has a pretty deep gash on his face and forehead. He was showing symptoms of a concussion, but he doesn't appear to have any swelling in the brain or anything, so that's good. He's heavily sedated right now, so he's not in much pain, but we need to get him to surgery immediately. We'll get his face stitched up and then start working on stabilizing and reconstructing that leg. We wanna let you go back and see him for a minute before we take him back for surgery. Do you have any questions or concerns for us?"

"I just want to see him," she said in a troubled tone.

"Okay, follow us. He's probably gonna be pretty groggy, but you'll be able to talk to him."

When Deborah got to the room where Jimmy was being prepped for surgery, she was saddened to see him in the hospital bed with tubes in his nose and arms, bloody bandages wrapped around his head and face, and his entire right leg elevated and wrapped up like a mummy. Although she knew he was going to be okay, it was hard for her to see her son in pain. Jimmy was a big and strong young man, and to see him in the hospital bed debilitated was staggering.

"Jimmy, look who's here," one of the nurses said.

"Hey, baby," Deborah said in a soft tone as Jimmy opened his eye that wasn't covered by the bandages.

"Hey, Ma." He labored.

"How you feeling?"

"I feel great," he joked and smiled the best he could while still laboring to speak.

"You're gonna be fine, baby. Just rest, they're gonna get you fixed up," she said as she patted his leg that didn't get injured.

"Okay, ma'am, we're gonna take him back. We'll take good care of him," the doctor said as the staff came in to wheel Jimmy's bed to surgery.

"Okay, let me say a prayer with him first."

Deborah grabbed Jimmy's hand, and they bowed their heads.

"Father, first and foremost, we want to thank *you* for saving Jimmy's life. Although he is hurt, it could have been worse, so we thank *you* that he is still here and doesn't have any injuries that he can't recover from. Now we ask that *you* watch over him as he goes through surgery. We ask for *your* presence in the operating room. We ask that *you* guide the hands of the surgeon and ensure that everything goes well. We thank *you* in advance for a successful surgery with no complications and for a healthy recovery. In Jesus's name, we pray. Amen."

"Amen," Jimmy said softly.

"Love you, Jim," Deborah said as she gave him a kiss

"Love you, Ma."

Deborah watched as they wheeled Jimmy out of the room and off to surgery. She knew he would be okay, but her heart was broken for him. She knew this would be a difficult road to recover physically, mentally, and emotionally. Jimmy was an impressive young man, but this was going to be one of the hardest things that he would have to go through up to this point in his life. It was going to be a true test of character.

CHAPTER 8

—— ❧ ——

Streetlights

Jimmy had multiple surgeries which lasted a combined total of six hours for procedures in which the surgeons repaired torn ligaments in his knee and fractures in all three of his major leg bones with metal rods and screws. After a few days of being heavily sedated on pain medication, Jimmy was slowly becoming conscious enough to entertain visitors. His mom, Deborah, had been staying at the hospital with him since the night of the accident, but he hadn't had any other visitors.

"Hey, Jim, Sean is on the way to come see you, if that's okay," Deborah said.

"Yeah, that's cool. Ask him to bring me Chick-fil-A. I can't force myself to eat any more of this hospital food."

"Okay, I will." She laughed.

"Tell him to get my usual. He'll know what to get."

"Okay, he said he should be here in about fifteen minutes."

"Cool. When did they say I could get out of here and go home?"

"Well, the doctor is supposed to be coming in soon to talk to us about that. I think they are expecting you to be ready for discharge tomorrow."

Right after Deborah said that, there was a knock on the door.

"Come in," Deborah said.

"Hey, buddy, how are you doing?" the doctor asked as he walked in.

"Not too bad considering my circumstance at the moment."

"I hear ya. Well, the procedures went well. The good news is that you didn't suffer any brain or organ damage. However, you dislocated your hip, fractured three bones in your leg, and had some ligament damage in your knee. There was no soft tissue damage in your hip, so getting that back in place didn't require surgery. But we did have to surgically repair the fractures to your femur, fibula, and tibia and hold them into place with a couple of metal rods and screws. Once we got your bones stabilized, we were able to get the ligaments in your knee repaired. And we also stitched up your face, which looked pretty good. It was extensive, but all in all, it went well. We didn't have any hiccups or unexpected issues."

"So, Doc, how long will I be out? Will I be cleared for summer workouts?"

"Look, Jimmy, our first hurdle is just getting you to walk again. That leg is gonna need a lot of time to heal before you can even put any weight on it. In my experience, people who suffer injuries such as yours tend to have nerve damage associated with it as well. So to be honest, that's gonna make it nearly impossible for you to play by next season…if ever. I would say if you are able to play again, you would be looking at maybe two seasons from now at the minimum."

Jimmy was speechless.

"Let's just focus on getting you healthy enough to do everyday tasks. Once we cross that bridge, we'll start working on getting you back into playing shape. I think you'll be good to go home tomorrow, and I'll send you home with some exercises that you can do while lying in bed to start activating those nerves and muscles that were damaged. Then when you start your physical therapy and rehab, you'll be doing some more challenging exercises to help you get back to normal. I know this is hard, buddy, but you're gonna be okay, I know you will. I'll be back a little later to check on you, but if you have any questions or concerns that the nurse can't answer, you can have her call me directly on my cell. Okay?"

"Thank you, sir. Thanks for your help," Deborah said.

"No problem. Hang in there, Jimmy," he said as he walked out of the room.

When the doctor left the room, Jimmy buried his face in his shirt and began to cry. He was not expecting to hear that news from the doctor, and he was crushed by it. Football had been his whole world and a huge part of his identity for most of his young life. His life was consumed with focusing, training, and practicing for football. Without the game that he loved, he didn't know how he would function or what he would do. The thought of never being able to play again was overwhelming. A week ago, he was playing in the biggest game of his life in front of thousands of fans and college scouts, and in the blink of an eye, things were drastically different.

"It's not fair." Jimmy sobbed.

"It's gonna be okay, baby," Deborah said as she tried to console him.

"I worked so hard, Ma. Now they're gonna pull my scholarship offers. Why did this happen to me? I don't deserve this," he said as he tried to pull himself together.

"I don't know, baby. But all things work together for the good of those who love God and are called according to His purpose. I know it's hard to see it right now, but God has a plan and a purpose for this. We just have to trust in His faithfulness."

"You're right. I can't see it right now. How can taking away the one thing I love work out for my good?"

"God loves you, Jim. He loves you so much that even though it breaks His heart, He's willing to walk with you through hell for a season in order to spend an eternity with you in heaven."

Jimmy couldn't see past his own frustration, so Deborah's words fell on deaf ears. He wasn't interested in trying to see things from a positive perspective after having his whole world turned upside down. He was angry and felt abandoned by God, whom he thought should have protected him from this type of misfortune.

Moments later, Sean arrived with Chick-fil-A in hand.

"What's up, bro? I got that number 2 with an Oreo milkshake for you."

"My man," Jimmy said with a smile as he wiped the tears from his face and sat up in his bed.

"Hey, Ms. Lawson. You been able to get some sleep?" Sean asked as he gave Deborah a hug.

"Hey, Sean. I've been sleeping okay. How are you feeling?"

"Sore but I'm okay. I should be out of this sling in a couple of weeks. Then I can start rehab."

"That's good," Deborah replied.

"How you feeling, Deuce?"

"I'm all right, man. The medicine they're giving me makes me groggy, but I'm not in too much pain."

"Cool. I know you're like the Wolverine. You'll be back on your feet in no time."

"I hope so." Jimmy laughed softly.

"So did they say they expect you to be cleared by the start of the season?"

"They just told me I might not ever be able to play again," Jimmy said in disappointment.

"What? Everything is going to be okay, bro. Don't worry, bro," Sean said as he fought to hold back tears.

Sean stayed with Jimmy for the rest of the day and helped him get his mind off of what the doctor said. Coach Thomas, Emily, and her mom also stopped by to hang out for a couple of hours. Jimmy may have lost the use of his leg temporarily, but his support system was still intact. He had his mom, good friends, and a coach whom he had a relationship with that extended far beyond the football field. Coach Thomas cared about him regardless of whether Jimmy was on his football team or not, and that is what Jimmy needed during this time of adversity.

The next day, Jimmy was released from the hospital but would have to spend the next several weeks getting around in a wheelchair. When he returned to school the following week, he struggled with having to depend on Sean and his other friends to help him get around and carry his tray at lunch. He was also self-conscious about the scar on his face and felt unsure of his identity now that he was no longer the best athlete in the school. Many of his classmates, including Samantha, did not know what to say to him and pretty much avoided him in school. After a few weeks of feeling like an outcast, it began to take a toll on him. He started skipping school, didn't want to go to church, and rarely left the house outside of going to rehab and physical therapy with Sean. The physical pain was slowly decreasing day by day, but mentally and emotionally, Jimmy was not doing well.

Rehab was also a frustrating and discouraging process for Jimmy. Just looking at the staples going up the side of his leg and the enormous amount of muscle atrophy was jarring. In addition to that, the scar tissue that developed in his leg from the surgery made the range of motion exercises extremely painful. He dreaded going to rehab, and each time that he went, he felt like he had regressed from the progress that he made in the previous session.

One Saturday following rehab, Jimmy came in the house, and his mom was in the kitchen cooking.

"Hey, Ma."

"Hey, Jim. I'm frying some chicken. You hungry?"

"Yeah, of course."

"Okay, it should be ready in about fifteen minutes. How was rehab today?"

"It sucked as usual. I feel like I take three steps forward just to take two steps back. I've been goin' for over a month now, and I've barely made any progress at all."

"Well, you're out of that wheelchair now, so you're making some progress."

"Well, not enough progress."

"Aw, don't get discouraged, Jim. You'll get there. Just keep praying and asking God to give you the strength to help you get back to normal as fast as possible."

"Ma, with all due respect, I don't wanna hear nothing about God right now. If God cared about me, He wouldn't have let this happen in the first place. I think I'm on my own with this one."

"'*From the rising of the sun unto the going down of the same the Lord's name is to be praised*,' Psalm 113:3. Whether you want to believe it or not, I know God has a greater purpose for your life. He allowed this to happen, not to harm you but to help you prosper into something that changes lives beyond the world of football. I know it's hard for you to see right now, son, but I know you'll get through this, and when you do, you'll see that God's plan for our lives will always exceed the expectations of our own."

Jimmy knew that his mom was right, but he felt like his whole world crumbled in a matter of moments in that car ride, and he didn't understand why God would take away everything that he worked for. All of the schools that had offered him a scholarship reached out to check on his well-being but ultimately reneged on their scholarship offers after news of the accident. They all said that they would still love for Jimmy to walk on and hopefully earn a scholarship once he recovered completely, but were unable to honor the initial offer due to the uncertainty of his ability to eventually return to the field. It was just one bad thing after another, and it was wearing on Jimmy's spirit.

Later on that evening, while Jimmy watched TV in his room, he got a text from Emily.

Hey are you home?

Yeah what's up?

Is it ok if I stop by?

Yeah sure

Delivered

Ok I'll be there in about ten mins

When Emily got to Jimmy's house, they hung out and talked for a little while, but Jimmy was unusually quiet, and visibly bothered.

"What's wrong, Jimmy? Why do you seem so distant?"

"I don't know. Just have a lot on my mind."

"Yeah, I get it. How have you been feeling? You still taking pain meds?"

"Nah, I've been off of those for a while. I'm not in any pain anymore. Just working to get my strength and mobility back."

"Oh, good. I know a lot of people—"

Jimmy cut her off in midsentence.

"Why are you here, Emily? What do you want from me? I'm a cripple, I got this ugly scar on my face. I don't wanna be mean, but I don't wanna be treated like a charity case. You don't have to come over here and check on me. I'm fine."

"Jimmy, you know I don't care about any of that. I never cared that you were a football star or that you are the most popular kid at school. I like you because you have a good heart, you've always been respectful to my mom, and you've always been nice to me. I never thought you let the high school celebrity thing go to your head, and I admired that about you. I don't have to be your girlfriend, but you're my friend, and I'm here for you no matter what."

Jimmy's insecurities had him in unfamiliar territory. He wasn't used to feeling so unsure of himself, but Emily's reassurance was comforting.

"I'm sorry, Em. I'm just having a hard time with all of this."

"I know. But you're a special guy. You'll get through it. '*Though I fall, I will rise, when I sit in darkness, the Lord will be my light*,' Micah 7:8. Sometimes God chooses His toughest soldiers to carry the heaviest load. It's tough, but it's an honor. God picked you to show the world His power."

Jimmy shook his head with a smile.

"You got this, Jim. I'm gonna get out of here. Save me a seat at church tomorrow, okay?" Emily said.

"Definitely." Jimmy smiled.

Emily left and Jimmy went to bed feeling much better. Emily helped him to see that he was more than just a football player to the people that knew him. His world had been consumed with football, but this experience was beginning to put things into perspective for him. Football was his passion, and he had God-given talent that was special, but his calling was bigger than football, and that was something that he was beginning to be thankful for.

CHAPTER 9

Hustle and Motivate

The next day, Jimmy woke up for church in much better spirits. He had been upset with God and hadn't been to church since the accident, but he was ready to stop blaming God and start seeking God's purpose in this circumstance. When his mom saw that he was getting dressed for church, she was encouraged. She had been praying every day that Jimmy would find peace and return to his faith, and it looked like her prayers were being answered.

"I'm happy that you're coming to church with me. I miss our usual Sunday routine," Deborah said as she helped Jimmy into the car with his crutches.

"You miss me driving you around." Jimmy laughed.

"It's not just that. But I'm glad you're coming."

"I still don't understand why God allowed it to happen, and I don't know if I ever will, but being mad at Him isn't going to make it any better."

"Yeah, you're right. Just trust Him. He has something great in store for you."

Jimmy and his mom made it to church, and Emily joined them just before the pastor took the stage to give his message.

"Today I will be preaching on the topic of Job. If you are unfamiliar with the book of Job, let me summarize it for you. Job lived in a town called Uz. He had ten kids, seven thousand sheep, three thousand camels, five hundred yoke of oxen, five hundred female donkeys, and a lot of servants. The Bible says he was the greatest of all the people of the East. Translation, Job was rich. He was wealthy. He had material things, and things money couldn't buy. But Satan accused Job of only serving God because He had blessed him with everything. So God allowed Satan to attack Job to prove to Satan that Job would praise the name of the Lord even in suffering. So one minute, Job had everything that you could ask for, and just like that, in a matter of days, he lost it all. His kids died, he lost all of his money and everything he owned. On top of all of that, he became extremely ill. Job was miserable, simply put, he hit rock bottom. Job says in chapter 3, verse 25, 'Everything I feared has come upon me.'"

He paused and then continued in a slow soft whisper, "So what do you do when you lose it all? Job was trying to figure out what he did to deserve this punishment. He had followed all of God's command-ments and was a good steward over everything that God had blessed him with. So why was God allowing all of these bad things to happen to Job?" He paused. "God wasn't punishing Job, He just wanted to take Job's faith to another level. He was actually promot-ing him. He was proud of Job, and it was time for Job to learn how to truly trust God. When everything in our lives is going wrong, God wants us to have peace, which lies in our faith in Him. When we know how much God loves us, it becomes easier for us to trust Him in spite of our current circumstances." He paused again and smiled. "Trust Him, He will never leave you or forsake you, His grace alone will bless you with much more than you could ever deserve. It's simply given to us because He loves us. Because Job trusted God in the midst of his nightmare, God rewarded Job by blessing him with twice as much wealth as he had before and allowed Job to live a long healthy life to enjoy it. So if there is anybody in the house that feels like their world is falling apart, and the walls are closing in on them, remember Job. Remember that even though Job was going through hell, God was with him every step of the way. Just like He did with Job, He will carry you through, all you gotta do is hold on."

Jimmy hadn't been to church in two months, and on his first Sunday back since the accident, the pastor delivered a message that related specifically to his circumstance. Jimmy knew that it wasn't just a coincidence, God was speaking directly to him, and it was exactly what he needed to hear. He needed to hear that God hadn't deserted him and that He was going to use his pain to be a blessing to someone else's life. There was still a long road to recovery lying ahead, but Jimmy was beginning to regain hope and put his trust back into God.

*****

Over the next few months, Jimmy and Emily began spending more time together. They started going to all of the youth church functions together, and Emily would text Jimmy motivational scriptures every morning. They would stay up on the phone with each other all night, talking and laughing. Jimmy had spent all of his free time playing sports and training over the last few years, but now that his injuries had him sidelined, he was enjoying being able to participate and help out with all of the activities at church.

Although Jimmy was only in high school, a lot of the kids at the church looked up to him, so he volunteered to be a peer mentor for the church's youth program. They got together once a week and played different games, conducted Bible study, and just talked about the challenges that they faced in their young lives. The elders at the church were thrilled to have a kid who was admired as much as Jimmy take on a leadership role among his peers.

Now that he had been getting out of the house more, Jimmy started to regain his confidence, and although he still wasn't physically back to normal, his quality of life was. He was back to laughing, joking, and having a good time like an ordinary teenager. As his spirits began to lift, he also made huge strides in rehab. He was still working to regain the strength that he lost in his leg, but he was back to walking again and had regained full range of motion. At this point, the rehab exercises were less painful and tailored more toward helping Jimmy return to his sports activities as soon as possible. After a few long months, he was finally climbing out of that dark hole that he was in. Although God's purpose had yet to be revealed to him, Jimmy's mom and Emily helped him to find joy and peace again in his life.

On the Saturday before Easter, Sean came to pick up Jimmy for rehab. When Jimmy got in the car, he looked at Sean and smiled.

"What?" Sean asked.

"Nothin', man, I just appreciate you for coming to rehab with me and being there for me over the last few months."

"Of course. '*A friend loves at all times and a brother is born for a time of adversity*,' Proverbs 17:17."

"*Oh*, so you've been in your Word, I see," Jimmy said, smiling and laughing.

"Yeah, a little bit. That accident was a wake-up call for me too, bro. We both coulda died that night, but God saved us and I'm grateful."

"No doubt."

"So what's up with you and Emily? That's your girl now?"

"I wouldn't say that. We're still just friends, bro. To be honest, I haven't had the courage to ask her to make it official, with this scar on my face and everything."

"Man, I was just about to tell you, that scar healed up nice. It makes you look tough. She's not worried about that."

"I hope you're right, but no need to press it. We're just hanging out."

"I feel you."

When they got to the rehab center, Sean started helping Jimmy with his stretches and balance exercises like usual. Once they were done stretching and warming up, the rehab trainer came in, and they began the strength exercises. Although he didn't have any leg injuries, Sean did the same exercises as Jimmy so that he could have a training partner. The strength training consisted of leg extensions, leg curls, lying lateral leg-raises, and pistol squats. The purpose was to rebuild the muscle in his injured leg that he lost during the time that his leg was in a cast and he was unable to use it. The intensity of these rehab sessions was not close to the intensity that Jimmy was used to training at, but nonetheless, they were just as challenging because of the muscle and nerve damage to Jimmy's leg. After about an hour of resistance exercises, Jimmy finished with ice and electrical stimulation to help reduce any inflammation that may have developed from the workout. While Jimmy and Sean were lying on the training table, Jimmy got his daily morning text from Emily.

"But those who trust in the Lord will renew their strength. They will soar high on wings like eagles. They will run and not grow weary. They will walk and not faint." Isaiah 40:31

Perfect scripture for a rehab day

Have a great workout 💪 🙏

As he read the text, one of the rehab center staff members came in with another guy.

"Hey, Jimmy, there's someone here that wants to see you," said the staff member.

"What's up, Jimmy? I'm Mike Hill, founder and CEO of Dawg Culture."

"How you doing, sir? Nice to meet you," Jimmy said as he shook his hand.

"Nice to meet you as well. I'm good, man, but I'm here to see how you're doing. I read an article about you the other day. I'm here at the rehab center talking to some of the kids in the cancer unit and wanted to come by to talk to you."

"Oh, about what, sir?"

"Well, a part of what I do is go around the country to different hospitals, rehab centers, and medical facilities to talk to patients about fighting through adversity. Back when I was in my early twenties, playing football, pursing my dream of playing in the NFL, I was diagnosed with stage 4 cancer, Hodgkin's Lymphoma. It got to the point where the doctors were telling me that there was nothing more that they could do, and I only had a few months to live. It was at that moment that I had to decide, was I gonna quit and give up on my life or was I gonna fight to stay alive. I chose to live and fight. I called upon that mentality that I had developed in football, and I approached my battle with cancer the same way.

"I woke up early and hit the gym when they told me I couldn't. I was lifting weights and putting on muscle when they told me I would start losing a lot of weight. I went in for my chemo and follow-up appointments and blew their minds every time they saw me. Of course I was feeling the effects of the chemo, but I kept fighting, I kept telling the doctors I'm a beast. I was determined to live, and that dawg in me is what kept me alive. My battle with cancer was cold, dark, and lonely, but I came out the other side a better man, a stronger man. So now my mission is to provide hope and inspire anyone else who is fighting something that seems impossible to overcome. Anyone who has been told that they only have a certain amount of time to live or anyone that's been told they will never walk again…or play again. It's time to unleash that dawg inside of you."

"No doubt. Thank you, sir. I appreciate the words of encouragement," Jimmy said, shaking his head and smiling.

"So what's up? Y'all gonna go win that state title this year or what?"

"The doctors said if I'm able to play again, it will probably take about two years because of the nerve damage," Jimmy said in disappointment.

"The doctors said," Mike Hill said, mocking Jimmy. "Jimmy, look at me, man. They told me I wouldn't be here right now. And if I would have just gone along with it and believed them, I wouldn't be. But you gotta believe in your own truth. First you see it, then you say it, and then you catch up to it. You gotta have that vision for yourself, then go get it. You a man of faith?"

"Yes, sir," Jimmy replied.

"That's good. So am I. Don't lose that faith. Hold on to it. That's your foundation. God will never leave you hanging. Trust me, I had some lonely nights, I know how it is. But He's there with you. He's the one who put that dawg in you for times like this."

Mike Hill reached in his book bag and threw Jimmy and Sean a T-shirt.

"I brought you guys a couple Dawg Culture tees for you to workout in."

"Thanks, this is dope," Jimmy said.

"When you put that shirt on, let it be a reminder of who you are and what you are. A dawg. All right?"

Jimmy nodded his head in agreement.

"Turn your pain into purpose," he said, looking at Jimmy in his eyes.

"Yes, sir."

"Good luck, fellas. I'll be looking for y'all to make some noise," Mike Hill said as he gave the guys a pound.

"Thanks, sir."

When Mike Hill walked out of that room, Sean looked at Jimmy and saw a fire in his eyes. He wasn't saying anything, but it was like something inside of him had been awakened, and his whole attitude and demeanor was being transformed by it.

"He's right, bro. We got unfinished business, and I ain't sitting out a whole year," Jimmy said with conviction.

"Welcome back. Let's run this back one more time." Sean smiled.

Sean was happy to hear Jimmy talk like that again. That was the Jimmy he knew and loved. A guy that believed he could do anything. A guy that was driven by doubters and naysayers. Jimmy was still physically limited, but what truly made Jimmy special was his passion and his will. With those things seemingly back to full strength, there was no limit to what Jimmy could do.

On that following Monday, after Easter, Jimmy and Sean woke up early and met at the track. The temperature was about fifty degrees, and the sun wasn't up yet, but there was just enough light peeking over the horizon for them to see. There was a light dew on the field, and there was a smell of fresh-cut grass in the air. It was the perfect day for Jimmy to begin preparing to make an unexpected early return to the field.

"You ready, bro?" Sean asked as they changed into their running shoes.

"I don't have my strength or explosiveness, but I'm cleared to train at full tilt. I'm more than ready to get back to doin' what I do best."

"Let's get it."

The guys began the workout with a four-lap jog for a warm-up. Jimmy had a little bit of a limp in his stride, but he wasn't in any pain at all. He felt awkward and slightly uncomfortable since it was the first time running in months, but he was elated to be doing it again after spending weeks in a wheelchair and another month and a half on crutches. Jimmy could remember the days a few months ago when he would lie in his bedroom, with his broken leg elevated, and daydream about being able to jog again. Although he was more out of breath than he expected, he jogged all four laps, holding back a grin due to his excitement.

After they completed the warm-up, they did a variety of ballistic stretches to prepare for the workout. Jimmy had to get back to the basics and rebuild his athletic foundation. He had to learn how to run all over again, so it was important for him to really focus on the detail in his sprinting mechanics. After stretching, they went onto the football field and did high knees, butt kicks, A skips, B skips, and carioca down to the twenty-yard line and back. The workout hadn't even started yet, and Jimmy had sweat dripping down his forehead. These drills that used to come so easy to him were now difficult to execute and required a high level of focus. Once they were done with the drills, Jimmy and Sean took a drink of water before starting the workout.

"All right, bro, we got sleds, chutes, and then we'll finish with one-hundred-meter sprints and abs," Jimmy said.

"All right, let's work," Sean said as he took a final drink of water and threw the bottle on top of his book bag.

They started the workout with six forty-yard sprints while dragging a fifty-pound sled. After sled sprints, they strapped on their speed parachutes and did six forty-yard sprints with those. Jimmy wasn't able to keep up with Sean, but he didn't allow that to discourage him. He kept grinding and pushing himself. They finished the workout with six one-hundred-meter nonresisted sprints and an ab circuit that included planks, flutter kicks, V-ups, and bicycles.

The next day, the guys went to the weight room and trained for two hours. The workout consisted of single-leg pistol squats, leg extensions, leg curls, hang cleans, and front squats. Wednesday's workout was field training. They worked on agility and change-of-direction drills using the agility ladder and speed hurdles. After they were done with the drills, Jimmy and Sean spent hours working on routes, timing, and chemistry. They spent the next two days training on the track and the weight room, but on Saturday morning, the guys drove out to Calvary Hill. Calvary Hill was a national park and popular hiking location up in the mountains, twenty miles outside of New Crofton. It was made up of three hundred acres of serpentine grasslands and dirt trails on a rugged mountainside. It was where Jimmy's track team used to practice when the coach wanted to punish them for something. Training at Calvary Hill was humbling. It had a way of breaking the will of most people, but Jimmy fed off of that challenge. He was the only one on the track team that liked training on the hill because he knew that it was just as much of mental exercise as physical.

"Yo, remember when Mike Hill came to talk to us at the center, and he said I had that dawg inside of me?" Jimmy asked Sean.

"Yeah."

"Well, this is where that dawg was born. On this hill. This hill separates the men from the boys and the lions from the men. It's gonna hurt, but we're gonna get through it together. And when it's over, we'll be one step closer to that goal."

Jimmy took off up the hill, and Sean followed behind him. Without stopping, they ran up the two-and-a-half mile hill at a steady pace. When they reached the summit, they were both sweating and breathing heavy, but the view over the park was stunning. The sun was shining, but there was a light cool breeze, the air was fresh, and it was quiet and peaceful. Lying next to a big boulder was a large tractor trailer tire with a rope and harness attached to it. "All right, bro, we gotta pull this tire for forty yards, five times, then back down the hill and back," Jimmy said as he strapped the harness around his waist.

"Jimmy, how much does this tire weigh??" Sean asked grudgingly.

"It's about two hundred pounds. Just drive, bro. Once you get the momentum goin', just keep driving until you cross that line."

"I got it. Let's go."

Pulling the tire was more than a workout, it was a test of will. It took power and strength to get the tire moving, but pulling it forty yards was a grind that took guts. Every step, every stride took 100 percent effort. The tire made them stronger, faster, more powerful, and more explosive, but it also made them tough and nasty. Jimmy believed that this is what set him apart from most of the other top athletes in the state. He believed that this torture that he willingly put himself through is what made him entitled to dominance on the field. There were plenty of guys with talent, but his passion for the game and determination are what fueled his engine.

Jimmy and Sean took turns pulling the tire back and forth, five times each, and then went back down the hill. Running up the hill this time with their legs feeling like jelly was torturous, but they didn't quit. They spent the whole afternoon pulling the tire and going up and down the hill, vomiting in between sets, and then getting right back to work. When they were done, they lay at the top of the hill in exhaustion. It was a great day of training to cap off the week, but the work was just getting started. The next week was the same, training Monday through Saturday on the track, weight room, field, and the hill.

Jimmy and Sean trained like this all summer. With fury, with passion, no days off, and no cheat days. This was the hardest either of them had ever trained. Jimmy always pushed himself physically, but what he had to overcome mentally was what made this off season the most challenging one of his life. At times, he would get discouraged, but he kept pushing and grew stronger and faster every day. In the beginning, he couldn't keep up with Sean, but by summer's end, they were neck and neck in every drill.

As the summer came to a close, Jimmy and Sean were in peak condition. They had done all they could to prepare for the season. Jimmy had worked to give himself a chance at making a comeback from a potentially career-ending injury, and Sean had worked to prepare himself to lead a team with significantly less talent back to a state championship. There were a lot of questions about what this Vickroy team would be without many of their key pieces from the previous season, but Jimmy and Sean were both ready to overcome the odds and answer all of those questions.

CHAPTER 10

─── ❧ ───

Sideline Story

Every year before the first day of training camp, everyone on the team is required to take and pass a physical performed by an approved medical physician. The purpose of the annual physical is for the student-athletes to demonstrate that they are capable and healthy enough to participate in a safe manner. Ordinarily, this was a task that no one lost any sleep over, but this year was different. When the news broke that Jimmy signed up to take his physical, every team in the state was anxious to hear the outcome. Although Vickroy graduated a lot of seniors that were key contributors to last year's team, a healthy Jimmy Lawson would put them right back into state title contention.

There had been rumors that Jimmy was making an attempt to be ready to play at the start of the season, but it was all just speculation up until the day of the physical. Although she had her concerns, Jimmy's mom knew how hard he worked to give himself a chance to make an early comeback, so she agreed that if he passed his physical, with no recommended limitations by the doctors, she would be okay with him playing in his senior season. Jimmy knew that he was healthy enough to play but was nervous that the doctors would place restrictions on him to protect themselves from any lawsuits in the event that he was reinjured.

Jimmy and Sean drove to the physician's office together and anxiously waited to be called back to see the doctor.

"You nervous, man?" Sean asked.

"A little bit," Jimmy replied with a laugh.

"Bro, if you aren't healthy enough to play, then no one on our team is. You've been beating me in sprints the last few weeks, so I think it's safe to say you're okay." Sean laughed.

"Yeah, I feel great. Just not sure if they'll fail me on some technicality or something."

"Nah, I think you'll be good, man."

"Sean Smith?" one of the physician's assistants asked.

"Yes, ma'am?"

"You can come on back."

"All right, bro. Cough cough and I'll be right back," Sean joked as he gave Jimmy a pound before heading to the examination room.

While Jimmy waited for his turn, he said a prayer, and a sense of peace came over him. Although there was nothing he wanted more than to pass his physical and be eligible to play in his senior year, he was beginning to trust God's will and plan for his life. He understood that God's plan was bigger and much more complexed than what he could see, and he was prepared to accept the path laid out for him.

A few moments later Sean came out with his results in hand and a big smile?

"How'd it go?" Jimmy asked.

"Piece of cake. Your turn," Sean said as the physician's assistant called Jimmy to come back.

"How are you today?" the PA asked.

"I'm well, ma'am. How are you?"

"I'm good. Thank you for asking. You can have a seat here and the doctor will be in to see you shortly," she said as she led him into the doctor's office.

Jimmy waited in the office for a few anxious moments and then in walked the doctor.

"Hey, Jimmy," the doctor said with enthusiasm.

"Hey. How are you?" Jimmy asked.

"I'm good. So this is a big day for you? I hold the power to the Pennsylvania state championship. I feel like a powerful man," the doctor said jokingly.

"Well, I don't know about all that." Jimmy laughed.

"I'm just kidding. How are you feeling? Do you think you're ready for full speed, full contact?"

"I feel outstanding. I've been training and working out at full speed for a couple of months now."

"Okay, good. Well, sit up on the table and let's take a look."

The doctor began the physical evaluation, checking Jimmy's lungs, eyes, and ears before testing his blood pressure and reflexes. Next was the intrusive hernia test. Jimmy didn't have any issues with those tests, but then it was time for the doctor to thoroughly check the condition of Jimmy's leg that had been theoretically reconstructed just months ago.

The doctor started with examining the stability in Jimmy's leg joints and making sure he didn't have any pain as he tested his range of motion. He then had Jimmy perform a series of lower body strength and mobility tests that he executed with ease. Jimmy had been doing weighted squats, lunges, and sprints all summer, so there was nothing the doctor could ask him to do that he would have difficulty with.

"Well, Jimmy, I'm impressed. If it weren't for the scars, I would have no idea that you were involved in such a serious accident."

"So does that mean I'm cleared to play?" Jimmy asked with excitement and anticipation.

"Yes, sir, I'm clearing you to play. Congratulations. You deserve it. You must have worked extremely hard to recover so fast from such serious injuries."

"I did, sir, thank you."

"Well, here is your letter clearing you for full participation. Good luck this season. I'll be watching," the doctor said as he gave Jimmy a handshake before walking him out.

When Jimmy got back out to the lobby, he had a look of disappointment on his face as he walked toward Sean.

"What happened, bro?" Sean asked in fear.

Then Jimmy looked at Sean with a smirk, winked, and said, "I'm back."

"Man, you almost gave me a heart attack," Sean said, holding his chest in relief.

As soon as they got in the car, Jimmy texted his mom, Emily, and Coach Thomas to tell them the good news. They all were anxiously waiting to hear from him and were elated to receive the good news that they hoped for.

Now that Jimmy was officially cleared to play, his eyes were set on returning to his dominant form and winning a state championship. Overcoming that first hurdle only made him hungrier and more confident. He believed that if he could prove the medical experts wrong and get on the field, there wasn't a player or a team that could stop him.

Although he surprised the doctors and physicians by passing his physical, he still needed more time to prepare for in-game action. He was able to participate in practice, but Coach Thomas didn't want him involved in full-contact drills just yet. They agreed to ease him back into things slowly to avoid reinjuring his leg by returning too soon. Since Jimmy was sidelined to start the season, other guys would have to step up to make up for the loss of his production.

EJ returned as Sean's go-to wide receiver, but there were a few new faces that filled other critical holes left by graduating seniors.

Danny Rogers was a junior wide receiver that had eighty catches and ten touchdowns on junior varsity in the previous season. He was a small and shifty guy with average speed and great hands. He was expected to give Sean a reliable target to go to on the opposite side of EJ.

Justin Simmons returned as the starting halfback. After being thrust into the starting lineup as a sophomore last year in the state championship game, he was confident that he was ready to have a more involved role in the offense this season. He worked hard in the off season and put on ten pounds of muscle. The local newspaper named him to the preseason all-district team, and everyone expected him to have a solid season.

On the defensive side of the ball, Vickroy had to find a replacement for Jimmy at free safety, starting linebacker Jeremy Rowley, and strong safety Tim Hall. Jeremy was the emotional and vocal leader of the defense, and there was no one on the team that could fill that role, but Matt Simpson, a junior linebacker that transferred from a school in Maryland, was one of the best athletes on the team. He was fast, athletic, and hit like a Mack Truck. The coaching staff was excited and optimistic about what he would bring to the defense.

Coach Thomas moved senior Brendan Bell, who didn't get any action as Jimmy's backup at free safety in the previous season to strong safety to replace Tim Hall. Bell was being recruited to play baseball in college, and he didn't possess the speed and explosiveness of many football players but what he lacked in athleticism, he made up for with intelligence on the field. Although he had his limitations, he was the perfect replacement for Tim Hall, who Coach Thomas described as the smartest kid he's ever coached.

Filling the shoes of Jimmy was sophomore Pete Davis. Davis was an absolute stud on junior varsity last year. He had twelve touchdowns and six interceptions in only seven games due to injury. He had a smaller frame and wasn't particularly durable, but when he was on the field, he was dynamic. He made the JV kids look like they were stuck in quicksand when chasing him around the field last year, and Coach Thomas believed he could do the same things on varsity this season if he stayed healthy.

Although the team was younger and less experienced than last season, Coach Thomas believed they had a shot to make the state playoffs due to a favorable schedule that was back-loaded. They started the season with easier opponents, and all of the schools that were expected to be good were scheduled toward the end of the season. This would allow Vickroy's young guys to build confidence, learn the playbook, and adjust to the speed of the game against teams that they were expected to beat. Then as players got more experience, they would be better prepared to face the tougher opponents.

Game 1: Highland High School

They opened the season with Highland High School who they beat 49–0 in the previous season. Highland was one of the smaller schools in the district and struggled to compete each year. They had a good coach and tough kids but couldn't match Vickroy's speed and athleticism last season. They expected things to be different this year since Vickroy wasn't as loaded with talent as they typically are. According to the local newspaper, the players at Highland had guaranteed a victory.

In the locker room before the game, Coach Thomas addressed the team.

"I'm gonna tell y'all right now, I'm pissed. You know why I'm pissed? Because I feel disrespected. We beat this team 49 to nothing last year, 38–6 the year before, 41–10 in the year before that. This team should not be on the same field with us, and they have the nerve to tell the *Morning Sun* newspaper that they guarantee a win? I don't care who we line up out there, they can't beat us. At Vickroy, we compete, we win. No matter what. That's our culture. Dominance. Yeah, we got one of our playmakers on the sideline, and we got some younger guys, but that doesn't change anything. I expect dominance tonight. I expect you to play with poise, discipline, fire, and intensity. Execute the game plan, play after play. We do that, same result as last year and the year before that and the year before that and the year before that! Let's go, men!"

Vickroy ran out of the locker room excited and anxious to prove that they were still a force to be reckoned with in the state. The first-year starters believed that they were just as good as the guys they were replacing, and they were ready to prove it.

Vickroy started out fast with Sean connecting with EJ on the first two plays from scrimmage for big gains of twelve and twenty-three yards. After establishing the passing threat, Coach Thomas turned to Justin Simmons to get the run game going and keep the Highland defense honest. On his first two carries, he showed off his extraordinary combination of quickness and power by making defenders miss in the backfield and then finishing with putting linebackers on their backs before being brought down for gains of ten and eight yards. On his third carry, Simmons received the handoff and burst through the hole up the gut. The free safety was the only one standing between him and the end zone. As Simmons attempted to make the safety miss in open field, another defender came from behind and ripped the ball out as he slung him to the ground. Highland jumped on the loose ball and recovered the fumble at their own thirty-yard line.

Highland's offense took the field and put together an impressive seventy-yard touchdown drive, keeping the Vickroy defense off balance with an effective combination of run and pass plays. On their next possession, Vickroy was able to respond with a long touchdown drive of their own, punctuated by Sean slicing up the defense in the air and on the ground.

When Highland got back on offense, Coach Thomas decided to run a dime defense to give his team an advantage against the pass in hopes that he would force Highland to be more one-dimensional. With only one linebacker on the field, Coach Thomas was putting a lot of faith in Matt Simpson to make plays, and he didn't disappoint. Play after play, he singlehandedly stifled the Highland run game with devastating hits. With so much uncertainty on the offensive side of the ball for Vickroy, Simpson was just what they needed on defense to keep them afloat.

Vickroy's offense struggled to find a rhythm, but on their final possession of the first half, Sean led them to another touchdown to give them a 14–7 lead going into halftime.

The second half was very similar to the first, with the Vickroy offense showing flashes of greatness but struggling to find consistency. On the defensive side of the ball, the dominance of Matt Simpson continued. Highland's offense went three and out on every possession but one in the third quarter due to back to back penalties on Vickroy. Early in the fourth quarter, Matt Simpson forced a fumble, and strong safety Brendan Bell was there for the scoop and score. The touchdown gave Vickroy a 21–7 lead and took the wind out of Highland. They played tough but knew it would take a miracle to come back from a two-touchdown deficit after being completely shut out for the majority of the game. As the game came to a close, both teams put their second-stringers in, and Highland was able to get a score as time expired to make the final score 21–13.

Coach Thomas was happy to get a victory, but a one-touchdown margin of victory against a team that hadn't had a winning season in years was undeniably a cause for concern. The offense struggled to find an identity without Jimmy, but it was up to Coach Thomas to find out what the strengths of his young team were and how to build an offensive scheme around those strengths. Fortunately for Vickroy, it was obvious that they had something special in Matt Simpson, and teams were going to have a hard time running the ball against them. Although it wasn't pretty, Vickroy survived week 1 without their best player, but there was still a long season ahead of them. If they wanted any chance of making it to the playoffs, they had a lot of improving to do.

Game 2: Eisenhower High School

In Vickroy's second game of the season, they faced Eisenhower High who they beat 48–6 in last year's matchup. Eisenhower went 4–6 in the previous season and had most of their starters return.

The game started as a defensive struggle, and the teams went into halftime with a score of 3–0 in Vickroy's favor. In the third quarter, Eisenhower scored two unanswered touchdowns to make the score 14–3 going into the fourth quarter. At the start of the fourth, Vickroy was able to get a crucial stop and made Eisenhower punt the ball with ten minutes left in the game. Down two scores, Vickroy got the ball and came out throwing. They moved the ball effectively with Sean hooking up with Danny Rogers for long gains on the first two plays and then connecting with EJ on a short slant route that he took to the house. When Eisenhower got the ball back, clinging on to a four-point lead, they tried their best to run the clock out to avoid giving the ball back to the Vickroy offense that seemed to hit its stride on their last possession. They didn't have much success running the ball with Matt Simpson in the middle of the field, but they kept converting on third down with short pass plays to keep the chains moving. Vickroy eventually got a stop on fourth down, but not before Eisenhower chewed the clock down to just over two minutes in the game.

Vickroy's offense took the field and put together a solid drive but turned the ball over on downs after a failed fourth down conversion attempt that ended with a wide-open dropped pass by the tight end. After turning it over and only one time-out remaining for Vickroy, all Eisenhower had to do was take a few knees and let the time run out. Vickroy took their first loss in the second game of the season to a team that was not expected to make the playoffs, and they were stunned. With Jimmy's return still uncertain, Coach Thomas had to figure out a way to generate more consistent offense, and he needed to figure it out immediately, or the season would be lost.

Game 3: Coldspring High School

In Vickroy's third game, they faced Coldspring High School, who they beat 24–0 in last year's matchup. Coldspring finished the season at 6–4 last year but got a new head coach in the off season and were off to a 2–0 start. Although it was still very early in the season, this game felt like a must-win for Vickroy. They could not afford to drop two of their first three games with the most difficult portion of the schedule still up ahead. Coach Thomas could sense that his team's confidence was wavering, and he feared that a loss this week could be a blow that they would not recover from.

The game was dominated by the defenses with Matt Simpson opposing his will on the Coldspring offense and Pete Davis providing two offensive touchdowns to give Vickroy a 17–14 win. It was great for Vickroy to get back into the win column, but things were not going to get any easier with a lot tougher opponents on the horizon. Vickroy needed to continue to improve each and every week to stay in the playoff hunt.

Game 4: Westview High School

In the fourth game of the season, Vickroy faced Westview High School. In the previous season, Vickroy pummeled Westview 42–7, but Westview was off to a 2–2 start this season, and they were hoping to make a playoff run themselves. This was a pivotal game for both schools and would be significant in determining each of their playoff chances.

Vickroy started fast, scoring touchdowns on their first two possessions, moving the ball mostly through the air on both drives, while Westview couldn't get anything going on offense in the first half. In the second half, Westview scored a touchdown on their first possession but barely made it past the fifty-yard line for the rest of the game. Vickroy pulled out their most impressive victory of the young season with a 24–7 win against a solid team.

Game 5: East Liberty High School

In the fifth game of the season, Vickroy faced East Liberty High School. In the previous season, Vickroy won the game by a score of 48–0, but East Liberty finished the season with a respectable 5–5 record. Although Vickroy was not having the success that they had in the previous season, they were still expected to win the game comfortably.

Sean accounted for all three of Vickroy's touchdowns, and East Liberty did not get on the board until the fourth quarter when all of the Vickroy starters came out of the game. As expected, Vickroy won the game handily and recorded its fourth win, improving their record to 4–1 on the year with a 22–8 victory.

Game 6: Joppatowne High School

In the sixth game of the season, Vickroy faced Joppatowne High School, who they beat 41–17 in the previous season. Joppatowne was 3–1 so far on the year and coming off of a bye week. The local newspapers predicted a close game but had Joppatowne as the favorite over a Vickroy team that they described as "having an identity crisis."

Joppatowne jumped out to an early 14–3 lead in the first quarter, but Vickroy was able to make the proper defensive adjustments and shut them out for the remainder of the game. Justin Simmons ran for 150 yards and a touchdown on the ground, and Sean accounted for 185 passing yards and a touchdown through the air to give Vickroy a 20–14 victory and improve to 5–1.

Game 7: Hamilton High School

In the seventh game of the season, Vickroy faced Hamilton High School, who they destroyed in the previous season 48–13 in a game that was expected to be much closer. So far this season, Hamilton was undefeated and looking for revenge.

The first quarter started out competitive with Vickroy and Hamilton scoring touchdowns on their first possessions, but Hamilton pulled away in the second quarter, adding two more touchdowns to take a 21–7 lead going into halftime.

At the start of the second half, Sean led his team on an impressive drive that was capped off with a spectacular catch by Pete Davis in the back of the end zone to cut the lead back down to seven points. Hamilton quickly responded with a touchdown drive of their own, stretching the lead back out to fourteen.

Vickroy couldn't get anything going offensively in the fourth quarter and were shut out for the remainder of the game. Hamilton went on to score another touchdown late in the game, making the final score 35–15 in favor of Hamilton, handing Vickroy their second loss of the season.

After the loss to Hamilton, Jimmy was itching to get back into the lineup. He wasn't back to 100 percent yet, but it had been killing him all season watching the offense struggle so much. He knew that his playmaking ability would add another dimension to the offense that teams would have a hard time defending. Immediately after the game, he went to the gym and trained for a few hours. The next week in practice, Jimmy participated in every contract drill and challenged his teammates to increase their intensity. He was ready to make his return and did not want to risk missing the playoffs when he knew he could be the difference-maker for his team, but after talking it over with Coach Thomas, they both decided that it was not in Jimmy's best interest to return just yet. Although he was anxious to help out the team, he wasn't quite where he needed to be for in-game action.

Game 8: Wheaton High School

In the eighth game, Vickroy faced Wheaton High School. They had trouble moving the ball against Wheaton in the previous season but were able to escape with a 21–6 victory. Wheaton's defense was always one of the best in the district, and this year was no different. They had an all-state linebacker and a cornerback that was in consideration for All-American honors. With the strength of Vickroy's team also being on the defensive side of the ball, the game was expected to be a defensive battle.

In the first half, Vickroy's defense played well, but their offensive struggles consistently gave the Wheaton offense good field position which led to a 10–0 Wheaton halftime lead. In the third quarter, Vickroy's offense was able to put together a drive that led to a field goal but gave up a touchdown which stretched the Wheaton lead to 17–3. Wheaton was able to control the ball for most of the fourth quarter and kept Vickroy off the board. A Wheaton field goal midway through the fourth put the game out of reach and gave Vickroy their second consecutive loss, bringing their record to 5–3 on the year. The season was slipping away, and Vickroy needed a big turnaround if they wanted a shot at making the playoffs.

Game 9: St. Martin's High School

After taking back-to-back losses, Vickroy's playoff chances were in peril. The good news was that with the season on the line, Jimmy was finally ready to make his debut. He knew that his team needed him, and if they wanted a shot at making the play-offs, they would need him to contribute in a major way in their remaining regular season games.

In Jimmy's first game back, Vickroy had to take on St. Martin's High School, who they beat 42–21 on homecoming in the previous season. Vickroy hoped that Jimmy would give them enough of a spark offensively to give them a slight edge over a solid St. Martin's team. But even with Jimmy back in the lineup, nobody expected them to win.

In the locker room before the game, it was evident that everyone had a little more confidence now that Jimmy was suiting up. They were all excited because they knew how much pressure Jimmy's presence would take off of everyone else. Just having him on the field made everyone's job a little easier. The running backs knew that the defense would be more focused on stopping the passing attack, and the other receivers knew that Jimmy would have the coverage rolled toward him, which would give them favorable matchups. Although Jimmy was just as excited as everyone else, he was also nervous. He hadn't played in a game all season, and the expectation was for him to pick up where he left off and dominate. The problem was that he wasn't so sure he could still do it. He was healthy and strong, but his confidence was still in the process of healing. Just before the team went out to the field, Jimmy received an encouraging text from Emily.

"My grace is all you need. My power works best in weakness."
2 Corinthians 12:9

Good luck 👍

Jimmy read the text and smiled. It was just what he needed to hear. Jimmy realized that his return wasn't just all about him. He knew that everything he did on the field moving forward would be for God's glory and not his own.

When the first quarter began, Sean tried to get Jimmy the ball early, but their timing and rhythm was off, so they struggled to get completions. While Vickroy struggled to find their way on offense, St. Martin's put together a drive that ended with their quarterback taking it in himself on a quarterback draw to take a 7–0 lead.

In the second quarter, Justin Simmons broke off a long sixty-five-yard run that put Vickroy inside the St. Martin's twenty-yard line, which led to a field goal and their first points of the night. When St. Martin's got back on offense, they responded with another touchdown drive, stretching their lead to 14–3 with two minutes left in the half.

Vickroy went back on offense, and Sean was able to orchestrate a two-minute drill well enough to get them into St. Martin's territory pretty quickly, but the drive stalled after two incompletions on dropped passes. They had to settle for a field goal to end the half. Although Jimmy's return didn't result in any offensive production as they hoped, Vickroy was happy to be within one score going into halftime.

Vickroy received the ball to start the second half and put together a drive that resulted in another field goal, making the score 14–9 early in the third quarter. When St. Martin's offense returned to the field, they had a drive that looked promising until Jimmy picked off pass intended for the tight end and returned it to midfield. Jimmy had been quiet in his return up until that point, but that was the kind of big play that everyone hoped to see from him. The third quarter came to a close with Vickroy punting the ball to St. Martin's, with the score still at 14–9.

At the start of the fourth quarter, the St. Martin's offense found success on the ground and was able to put another touchdown on the board to increase their lead to 21–9. Although St. Martin's had a firm lead, with ten minutes remaining and only being down two scores, Vickroy still had a shot to win the game.

When Vickroy got back on offense, they started the drive off with a screen pass to Jimmy in which he stiff-armed a defender and took off for a thirty-yard gain before being forced out of bounds. On the next play, Sean connected with Jimmy again for a twenty-yard gain on a corner route. On the following play, Justin Simmons gained another twenty yards on a halfback draw which put Vickroy inside the St. Martin's five-yard line. On the next play, Sean threw a jump ball up to Jimmy, who had one-on-one coverage on the outside, and he was able to bring it down for Vickroy's first touchdown of the game, which cut the deficit down to five points and a 21–16 score.

When St. Martin's got back out on offense, they were feeling the pressure with Vickroy now within one score of taking the lead. They attempted to run the ball all the way down the field to drain the clock, but Matt Simpson and the Vickroy defense was suffocating the St. Martin's running game. Not being able to get the run game going, St. Martin's had to punt the ball to Vickroy with three minutes left in the game.

Vickroy started the drive with a quarterback draw in which Sean was able to pick up ten yards. On the next play, Sean connected with EJ on a curl route for an eight-yard gain. On the next two plays, Justin Simmons carried the ball and was able to pick up two first downs. With under a minute left in the game, the Vickroy offense came out in their empty package to get five receivers on the field. Sean completed passes to EJ and Pete Davis on the next two plays and used a time-out to stop the clock. Lined up on the St. Martin's twenty-yard line, Vickroy came to the line of scrimmage in a single back formation with Jimmy lined up as the slot receiver to the right. Sean got under center, signaled for EJ to come in motion, and hiked the ball. Sean handed the ball off to EJ on a jet sweep, and then EJ handed it to Jimmy on a reverse, going back in the other direction. With the St. Martin's defense in pursuit, Jimmy turned on the jets and sprinted to the end zone for the game-winning touchdown. St. Martin's was stunned. They did a good job of containing Jimmy for the entire first half, but they weren't able to get a stop when they needed it most. The excitement on the Vickroy sideline was through the roof because they knew that with Jimmy playing the way that he did in the second half, they had a chance to beat any team they faced. Deuce was back, and every team in the state was worried.

After the game, all of the local newspaper reporters were lined up to get an interview with Jimmy.

"Jimmy, what a season debut. An interception, a receiving touchdown in the third, and a game-winning rushing touchdown in the fourth. It must feel great to be back, healthy again."

"Well, I'm not 100 percent yet, but I'm getting there. It definitely did feel great to be back out there with my guys. Y'all don't know how much it was eating me up inside to watch from the sidelines," Jimmy said, laughing.

"When you first got into the accident, I remember hearing that the doctors didn't believe you would be able to play again. Can you tell me about the work that you put in that allowed you to be out there with your teammates once again?"

"Well, I worked hard, but it was really the grace of God that allowed me to come back this season. I couldn't be back out here without Him."

"Well, you sure have an inspiring story. Good luck the rest of the season, Jimmy."

"Thanks. God bless."

With that comeback win, Vickroy was 6–3 and still alive in the playoff hunt. With Jimmy Lawson back, there was no telling how far they could go.

Game 10: Merryville High School

In the last game of the season Vickroy had to face Merryville, who they beat 28–0 in the previous season. With a 6–3 record, Vickroy was in a position to secure a spot in the playoffs with a win, but it wasn't going to be easy. Merryville was already headed to the playoffs with a 7–2 record but looked to pick up another win to improve their seed.

The Vickroy defense had been playing well for most of the season, so coming into the game, Coach Thomas's game plan was to slow the game down by running ball, and that's just what Vickroy did. They started the game by running the ball on every play of their first possession, which led to a twenty-yard field goal and an early 3–0 Vickroy lead. Vickroy's defense shut out the Merryville offense in the first quarter, but a questionable pass interference call midway through the second quarter led to a Merryville touchdown on a short outside run by the quarterback. On Vickroy's final possession of the second quarter, they were able to chew up most of the time remaining in the half on a long twenty-play drive that consisted of seventeen runs and only three passes. They capped off the drive with an eight-yard touchdown run by Justin Simmons where he showed off his athleticism by hurdling a defender on his way to the end zone.

Vickroy led with a score of 10–7 going into half-time, but at the start of the third quarter, Merryville threatened to retake the lead with long pass completions on their first two plays. With the ball on the Vickroy thirty-yard line, Merryville ran a quarterback option, but it was quickly stopped for no gain. On the next play, Merryville went back to the passing game and threw a pass over the middle to the tight end, but it was intercepted by Brendan Bell, who was brought down immediately after the pick.

For the remainder of the third quarter, neither team was able to attain any significant offensive production, and the quarter expired with the score remaining the same at 10–7. The fourth quarter began with Vickroy's offense on the field looking to put together a drive to give them their first points of the second half. Coach Thomas stuck with the running game, and they ran the ball on seven consecutive plays as they drove into Merryville territory. Although they didn't have any plays for large gains on the ground, the steady run game of Vickroy was beginning to wear the Merryville defense down as the game went on. Justin Simmons was beginning to find his groove, and with about eight minutes left in the game, he scored his second touchdown on a short three-yard run to the right side of the field to give Vickroy a 17–7 lead.

On the ensuing kickoff, Merryville returned the kick for a touchdown and cut into the Vickroy lead, making the score 14–17 midway through the final quarter. Although Vickroy's lead was slim, they were confident that they could close the game out barring a catastrophic mistake. On their next possession, Vickroy took their time and pounded the ball down the field three yards at a time and ran the clock out to win the game. The 14–17 victory gave Vickroy a 7–3 record for the regular season and locked them in for a playoff berth. They were all excited to get another opportunity to play in the playoffs, but now that Jimmy was back, they had their eyes on much more.

Heading into the playoffs, Central Catholic was undefeated again and the favorites to go back to back as state champions. They hadn't lost a game in two years, and although they had lost their best players from the previous season, they had reloaded on both sides of the ball and were just as dangerous. Replacing Adam Sanchez at quarterback was a junior named Jodi Moore with a big 6'5", 230-pound frame, and a big arm. He didn't have the running capability that Sanchez had, but he had elite arm talent that already had college coaches salivating. He also had a more dynamic set of receivers to throw to with a pair of transfers from New Jersey, Johnson and Allen, joining the team in the off season. At running back, they replaced last year's state championship MVP, Kevin Jones, with Austin Lott. Lott was another game-changing back that could do it all. The offensive linemen were all 275 pounds and up, and they were all seniors heading to college with football scholarships. They were dominant all season and made the Central offense extremely versatile. With one of the best offensive lines in the whole country,

Central had the option to pound the ball down the entire length of the field or let Moore sit back in the pocket and pick apart the secondary through the air.

They weren't as physical on the defensive side of the ball as they were in the previous season, but they were the fastest defense in the state. One opponent described the Central secondary as "omnipresent" because they seemed to be everywhere on the field. Because the secondary was so talented, Central Catholic was able to send pressure with blitzes on the majority of their defensive plays. This made it very difficult to find running lanes and left very little time for opposing quarterbacks to find open receivers, which was the reason why Central led the state in interceptions during the regular season.

There are no guarantees in playoff football, but everyone in the state knew that taking down a juggernaut like Central Catholic would be nearly impossible. It would be a miracle if they were somehow knocked off before making it to the championship game once again. Luckily for Vickroy, although they were one of the lower seeds in the playoffs, they were placed on the opposite side of the playoff bracket which meant that they wouldn't have to worry about facing Central until the championship game, if they were able to make it there.

First Round of Playoffs: Beaver Dam High School

In the first round of the playoffs, Vickroy faced the number 3 seed, Beaver Dam High School, who finished the regular season with a 9–1 record. Beaver had an impressive defense with three all-state seniors in the defensive front seven. They were fast and physical. Throughout the year, they recorded five shutouts, and no team had scored more than seventeen offensive points against them.

The game began with Vickroy receiving the opening kickoff. On their first possession, Vickroy moved the ball against the strong Beaver defense and scored a touchdown on a deep crossing pattern to Pete Davis. The rest of the first half was defensive tug-of-war as neither team was able to score any more points before halftime.

In the third quarter, Vickroy scored another unanswered touchdown to take a commanding 14–0 lead before the start of the fourth quarter.

The fourth quarter was much like the first three, with Vickroy scoring a touchdown on a long drive that was capped off with an eight-yard run by Justin Simmons. Beaver was finally able to get on the board with a touchdown with one minute left in the game, but it was too little too late. The game ended with a final score of 21–7. It was a huge upset as most of the papers predicted Beaver to be a final four playoff team.

After all of the talk about how good Beaver's defense was, it was the Vickroy defense that stepped up to the challenge. Not many people expected Vickroy to make it to the playoffs, and even less people thought they would win any playoff games. But with a pretty convincing upset win in the first round, they had gotten the attention of every other playoff team.

Second Round of Playoffs: Hamilton High School

In the second round of the playoffs, Vickroy had to face a familiar opponent, Hamilton High School. They suffered an embarrassing 35–15 loss to Hamilton in week 7 of the regular season, but that was before Jimmy returned from his injury. To ensure that Jimmy would have a significant impact on the game, Coach Thomas designed a package of run plays with Jimmy in the backfield for the rest of the playoffs. Football is a team game, but a player with Jimmy's talent could completely change the outcome of any game with a few big plays. Vickroy knew that, and they were confident that the outcome of this game would be different from the last.

The first quarter began with Hamilton receiving the kickoff. They were able to quickly move the ball down the field and score a touchdown. Vickroy immediately responded with a touchdown of their own on their first possession. As the first quarter came to a close, Hamilton moved closer to regaining the lead by completing a long pass to get inside the Vickroy ten-yard line. When the second quarter began, the Hamilton offense didn't waste any time, punching it into the end zone to take a 14–7 lead.

When Vickroy got back on offense, they used the majority of the time remaining in the half to put together a methodical eighteen-play drive that ended with Jimmy taking a handoff up the middle and scoring on sixteen-yard run to tie the game up at fourteen going into the half.

In the third quarter, the teams traded touchdowns again to bring the score to a tie at twenty-one points. Both offenses were rolling, and it looked like the game was going to come down to whoever had the ball last. In the fourth quarter, Vickroy was able to strike first with a touchdown on an eight-yard quarterback scramble to take their first lead of the game. The Hamilton offense didn't take long to respond, scoring a touchdown on a fifty-yard run by their talented running back, tying the score again at twenty-eight.

Vickroy got the ball back with four minutes left. Hamilton hadn't been able to stop them all game, and they were confident that they would have no problem moving the ball down the field to score with the game on the line.

Vickroy started the drive with a screenplay to Justin Simmons that went for eighteen yards. On the next two plays, Jimmy carried the ball for short gains. Facing a third and long, Vickroy came out in an empty formation and threw the ball to Danny Rogers on a post for a first down. With the game clock under two minutes, Sean threw the ball on a checkdown to Justin Simmons, who was able to pick up a first down inside the Hamilton forty-five-yard line. On the next two plays, Sean attempted to connect with EJ, but Hamilton forced incompletions with tight coverage. On third down, they ran a bootleg with Sean rolling out to the right, giving him the option to throw to a receiver toward the sideline or pick up yards with his legs. Seeing no receivers open, Sean took off down the sideline, made one defender miss with a jump cut, and shrugged off another with a stiff arm before being brought down at the Hamilton twenty-yard line. Not wanting to settle for a field goal, Vickroy stayed aggressive, and on the next play, Sean connected with Rogers on a corner route for a sixteen-yard gain. Now inside of the five-yard line, Vickroy ran the ball on three consecutive plays to punch it in for a touchdown, with hardly no time remaining on the clock, and avenged one of their worst losses of the season.

Vickroy won the game with a final score of 35–28. In an offensive shootout, Vickroy was able to secure another upset victory in the playoffs. They were on their way to the semifinal round of the playoffs, and they were proving that they belonged there.

Semifinal Round of Playoffs: Independence High School

In the semifinal round of the playoffs, Vickroy had to face Independence High School. Independence was another Cinderella team that snuck into the playoffs and had beaten two top seeded teams in the first two rounds. Much like Vickroy, they didn't care who the favorite was. They believed that they would be able to find a way to win in the end. They had a dangerous combination of confidence and hunger, and the only way Vickroy would be able to win was if they brought that same energy to the game.

Independence received the ball to start the game, and Vickroy forced a quick three and out. When Vickroy got the ball, they moved the ball down the field well, but the drive came to a halt after Justin Simmons fumbled the ball inside of the Independence twenty-yard line. On Independence's next drive, they threw an interception that was returned for a touchdown, which gave Vickroy a 7–0 first-quarter lead.

In the second quarter, both offenses traded touchdowns to bring the score to 14–7 going into the half. Vickroy received the ball to start the third quarter and had to punt after Independence forced three straight incompletions on pass plays. When Independence got on offense, they put together an impressive touchdown drive to tie the score at fourteen.

Vickroy got the ball back, and on the last play of the third quarter, they scored on a long pass play to Jimmy on a post route. The fourth quarter was mostly a defensive battle with neither team being able to generate much offense. As time in the game was beginning to expire, Independence got desperate and forced a throw into double coverage which resulted in another pick six for Vickroy and sealed the victory for them. They won the game 28–14 and were on their way to the state championship. No one expected them to be there, but they were as dangerous as anyone and believed they could win, no matter who they faced.

Shortly after the game, Vickroy was informed that Central Catholic won their semifinal game. Which meant that they would be the team Vickroy had to face in the state championship game. Although everyone from Vickroy already expected to face Central, when it was finally confirmed, everyone immediately stopped celebrating and began mentally preparing for the challenge ahead.

CHAPTER 11

— ∞ —

We Go High

In the week leading up to the state championship game versus Central, Vickroy had a great week of practice. They hadn't lost a game since Jimmy returned to the team, and now that he had been back for five weeks, the team was back into a rhythm. The offensive scheme was built around Jimmy's playmaking ability, and the defense was built around the speed and physicality that Matt Simpson had been bringing all year. They had been playing disciplined football all season and didn't have many penalties. They knew that if they continued that in the state championship game, they had the playmakers that could compete with Central's. With Jimmy back in action, everyone was healthy, and most of the starters had state championship experience. For the players that played in last year's game, they remembered what that loss felt like, and they were ready for revenge.

The day of travel to Hershey for the state championship game was similar to the year before. The team all boarded the bus early in the morning on Friday and took the two-hour trip to the Hershey compound. Once there, the team checked in to the hotel and then rode over to the stadium to do walk-throughs. Once walk-throughs were finished, Coach Thomas let the players go to their rooms and relax before team dinner. It was exciting to be back at Hershey again for the state championship game, but Jimmy, Sean, and the rest of the seniors on the team were there for business. Although their presence in the championship game was an accomplishment in itself, the mission would not be complete without a victory. After team dinner, Jimmy and Sean went to the field one last time before going back to their hotel rooms. Instead of taking mental reps, like they usually did, they sat in the bleachers and just talked.

"You know what's funny? Last year, we were loaded, undefeated, didn't even have any close games, and I was still nervous when we got here. This year, we might not be as talented, but I know we're gonna win tomorrow," Sean said.

"I feel the same way, bro. This team has shown that no matter what, we're gonna keep fighting. I like that about this team."

"Yeah, man. Last year, we didn't know what it was like to be in a close game, so when it came down to the wire, guys got tight."

"This year, all our games have been close," Jimmy said, laughing.

"If we're in it in the end, they're the ones that are gonna get tight. We'll be the ones that are comfortable."

"That's where we'll have the advantage."

"Yup, just gotta play disciplined ball in the first half. Don't give up big plays, don't commit penalties, don't turn the ball over," Sean said.

"We got this one, bro. We're gonna shock the world."

Jimmy and Sean sat on the bleachers for an hour and reflected on their season and the past year. Their high school careers had plenty of ups and downs, joy and pain, and what they had been through in the past twelve months had made them better young men and gave them a stronger bond. They had accomplished a lot in their high school careers, and although they looked forward to playing in college, knowing that they only had one more game in high school was bittersweet.

The next day, the guys had team brunch in the hotel and then went back to their rooms for a few hours before heading over to the stadium. When the team arrived at the stadium, they put on their equipment and went out to the field to warm-up. After warm-ups, everyone went back into the locker room. Most guys put on their headphones and listened to music to get themselves in the zone, some went over their playbooks, but Jimmy went to his locker, got on his knees, and said a prayer.

"Father, thank you for the blessing of being here today. Thank you for giving me the opportunity to play in this game when they told me I may never play again. I ask for your protection for everyone out on the field tonight, and I also ask for your favor, but more importantly, I ask that you give me the strength to honor you in either victory or defeat. I ask that you help me to play with discipline, focus, and intensity, but do it all with class, respect, and humility. I know you are faithful, and all my trust is in you. In Jesus's name. Amen."

Shortly after Jimmy finished praying, Coach Thomas walked in the locker room.

"Bring it in tight. All eyes on me. All right, listen up. I started playing this game when I was eight years old. I played in boys' and girls' club, played in high school, played as an undergrad in college, played as a graduate transfer in college, took my shot in the NFL, and after that didn't work out, I've been coaching ever since. I love this game. This game has been a part of my life for as long as I can remember, and it has taught me so much. How to work hard, how to be disciplined, how to work with other people, how to bounce back and overcome adversity… it taught me how to be a man. This is a man's game. When you play this game, you play with passion, you play with fire, you play with hunger, you play with pain…play with confidence, courage…be intense… or don't play at all. This game ain't about finesse, and it ain't for pretty boys that don't wanna get dirty and bleed for a victory. That's what has gotten us this far.

When nobody believed we would or should be here, we imposed our will on every team that we needed to beat to get here. We wanted it more than them and were willing to do what they weren't willing to do to make it happen. Now here we are again tonight, facing a team that everyone thinks is better than us. So what? Nothing new for us. Business as usual, right? For those of us that were on the team last year, we all remember what we felt like on the losing end of this last year, right? It hurt. I couldn't sleep for two weeks after that loss, and honestly, I'm still not over it yet. It still hurts, and I'm sure some of you feel the same. Now how bad do you wanna get rid of that pain? How bad do you wanna get rid of that pain? Forty-eight minutes, that's all it takes. Forty-eight minutes, four seconds at a time. Four seconds, reload, four seconds, reload. Leave everything you got out on that field tonight. No regrets. That's all you need to worry about. You read your keys, you play with more effort than them, one play at a time. Stack! Stack! Stack! Stack! Stack! Stack! Win!"

Everyone in the locker room went wild.

"Win on three, win on three. One, two, three."

"Win!"

Vickroy bust out the locker room and into the tunnel. They were on fire and ready to play in the game of their lives.

When the team ran out of the tunnel, Central Catholic was already out on the field, and the stadium was packed to capacity with thirty thousand fans. Jimmy ran out on the field, took a deep breath, and took it all in. He had been told before by his coaches and former players that there was no level of football like high school football, and that he would surely miss it when it was all over, so he wanted to take one final moment to appreciate it all before kickoff.

Before the coin toss, the teams stood on their sidelines and took their helmets off for the national anthem. After the national anthem was complete, the captains went to the center of the field for the coin toss.

Central Catholic won the toss and elected to defer to the second half, so Jimmy and the Vickroy return team went out on the field to receive the opening kickoff. As Jimmy ran out on the field, Coach Thomas yelled to get his attention.

"Deuce. It's showtime."

"You already know, Coach," Jimmy said with a smile.

Once Jimmy got set, he softly patted his chest and pointed to the sky to acknowledge God. All the fans in the stadium stood to their feet as Central Catholic lined up for the kickoff. The energy in the stadium was palpable, and the fans were anticipating a game full of highlights, just like last year's matchup. Central kicked the ball deep to the back of the end zone, Jimmy caught the ball, took a knee, and tossed it to the ref. Central believed that they were by far the better team, but they weren't stupid enough to give Jimmy the opportunity to return the opening kickoff for a touchdown. They believed that they had enough talent to win, even if they played conservatively.

The Vickroy offense jogged out to the field and got in the huddle. Sean took a knee and commanded the offense.

"Disciplined and physical. Controlled rage. That's what we're bringing all night. Let's set the tone on this first drive. Power right, 28 zone on one, on one. Ready."

"Break!"

The Vickroy offense came to the line of scrimmage in a power I formation, with Jimmy lined up in the backfield along with two lead blockers. Sean got under center and quickly hiked the ball. Jimmy took the handoff and bounced it to the outside, running with his hand on the back of his lead blocker. With the defense in pursuit, Jimmy made a sharp cut up the field inside of the block to pick up about twelve yards before being brought down by the Central Catholic safety.

On the next play, Vickroy ran a quarterback draw, but it was stopped for a short gain. On second down, Sean completed a pass to Danny Rogers on a comeback in which he was able to shake a defender and gain about fifteen yards after the catch. It gave Vickroy a first down and put them at midfield. On the next three plays, Justin Simmons carried the ball on three consecutive downs and was able to pick up another first down. The Vickroy offense was moving the ball down the field slow and steady, just as they hoped they would. The Central Catholic defense was fast and well coached, so Coach Thomas knew that physical, slow, and methodical drives would be the only way to generate points. On the next play, Vickroy tried to catch the Central Catholic defense off guard with a play-action fake to the running back, but Central sent a middle linebacker blitz which disrupted the entire play and landed Sean six yards deep in the backfield for a sack.

Facing a second and long, Vickroy came out in a shotgun spread formation, with Jimmy lined up in the backfield and attempted to run a halfback screen, but it was sniffed out by the Central defense, and he was tackled at the line of scrimmage for no gain. On third down, Vickroy came out in an empty formation and threw the ball to Pete Davis on a slant, which he took up field for a twelve-yard gain, but it was not enough for a first down, which forced a punt on Vickroy's first drive.

Central received the punt at their ten-yard line and returned it thirty-five yards to the forty-five-yard line after a Vickroy defender made a touchdown-saving shoelace tackle. On Central's first offensive play, they handed the ball off to the running back, Austin Lott, who took the ball straight up the middle for a four-yard gain and was brought down after a vicious collision with Matt Simpson in the middle of the field. On the next play, Lott carried the ball to the outside and was able to outrun the Vickroy defense around the edge and pick up a first down before being pushed out of bounds at the Vickroy forty-yard line. On the next play, Central showed off their ability to pass after coming out in a shotgun trips formation and completing a pass to a receiver on a corner route for a fifteen-yard gain. It was clear that the Central Catholic offensive play caller was trying to show an ability to move the ball effectively on the ground and through the air early to keep the Vickroy defense off balance throughout the rest of the game. On the next play, Central lined up in the shotgun trips formation again and gave the ball to Austin Lott on a draw play which he took all the way down inside of the Vickroy ten-yard line. After the tackle was made, Central Catholic hurried to the line of scrimmage without getting into the huddle.

"Slingshot, slingshot!" the Central quarterback, Jodi Moore, yelled from under center.

Before the Vickroy defense could get into position or make any adjustments, Central snapped the ball and completed a pass on a quick slant for a touchdown. The Central Catholic offense moved the ball down the field with ease and were out to an early 7–0 lead midway through the first quarter.

When Vickroy got back on offense, they went back to the power I formation and attempted to establish the running attack with Jimmy and Justin Simmons. Coach Thomas was trying to stay away from the strength of the Central defense and keep the ball on the ground, but the aggressive blitz from Central forced the Vickroy running backs to break tackles in the backfield before they even got back to the line of scrimmage.

Vickroy slowly inched the ball down the field three yards at a time, but it was clear that Central was content with letting them grind out yards the hard way, knowing that one sack or tackle for loss would put Vickroy in a position that would force them to throw at their spectacular secondary. After picking up a first down on a remarkable run by Jimmy, in which he took a handoff on an outside zone play, reversed field, and outran the entire front seven of the Central defense to pick up twenty-five yards before being tackled, Vickroy lined up in a shotgun spread formation as the game clock in the first quarter winded down. Sean could see that the Central linebackers were inching up to come on another blitz, and the cornerbacks were lined up directly in front of the receivers in press man coverage. Sean patted the top of his helmet and yelled, "Big top, big top," indicating the offensive play call to his teammates.

As soon as the ball was snapped, Central brought the pressure up the middle as Sean expected. Sean caught the shotgun snap and immediately heaved it up, down the right sideline to EJ, whom he trusted to beat one-on-one coverage any day against anybody. The Central defender was in tight coverage, but EJ was known to consistently win in jump ball situations. As the ball came down around the Central ten-yard line, EJ jumped up with two hands and caught the ball, but as he came down, the Central defender ripped the ball out of his hands and went running up the sideline the other way as EJ fell to the ground. The Central defender cut across the field, weaving through Vickroy players, and returned the ball for a touchdown as the clock expired in the first quarter to take a 14–0 lead.

Vickroy was stunned and exhausted. Central was up by two touchdowns, and it felt like they had exerted very little effort thus far. But this Vickroy team was battle-tested. They had been down before, and they knew that if they just kept fighting, they would have an opportunity to turn the game around.

With Vickroy receiving the kickoff at the start of the second quarter, Coach Thomas had to figure out a way to move the ball more effectively. If they weren't able to get points on the next drive, he knew how difficult it would be to prevent Central from increasing their lead to three scores before halftime.

"If they are gonna keep sending pressure, we gotta be able to take advantage of that and execute on these screen passes. Everyone has to do their jobs and make their blocks. Once we gash them a few times, they'll have to back off a little bit," Coach Thomas said to his players in the huddle before the offense took the field.

On the first play from scrimmage in the second quarter, Vickroy snapped the ball and immediately threw the ball to EJ on a wide receiver screen, but he was unable to gain any yardage due to the press coverage of the Central defenders. On the next play, Sean threw the ball to Justin Simmons on a halfback screen, and he was able to rip off a big twenty-yard gain. Coach Thomas anticipated that Central would eventually ease up on the pressure, but they continued to bring the blitz, play after play. On the next two plays, Sean quickly dumped it off to Jimmy in the flats, and he was able to pick up two first downs.

On first and ten, from the Central thirty-six-yard line, Vickroy went back to the running game and let Simmons carry the ball off tackle for a short gain. On the next play, Vickroy lined up in an empty formation, and Sean attempted to get the ball to Danny Rogers on a deep crossing pattern, but the pressure forced the ball to be overthrown, and it landed incomplete. On third and long, Vickroy attempted another screenplay, but the Central defense anticipated the play, read it well, and was able to make the tackle after a short gain, which brought Vickroy to a fourth and three from the Central twenty-nine-yard line. On fourth down, Coach Thomas decided to kick the field goal, and they were able to convert to get their first points of the game and make the score 14–3.

When the Central offense returned to the field, they lined up in the I formation and ran the ball on each of their first six plays. They marched the ball down the field and ate up the clock as they went. Although the first half was almost over, the Central offense had barely been on the field, and they were still fresh. Most of Vickroy's defensive players were also offensive players, and they were gassed from the long offensive drive. Vickroy was on their heels, and Central knew it. They continued to play smash-mouth football and consistently picked up four to five yards on every play. Vickroy knew what was coming, but they were too tired to stop the physical offensive line of Central from blowing them off the ball on every play. As the game clock in the second quarter continued to wind down, Central came to the line of scrimmage, let the play clock get down to one second, hiked the ball, and gave it to their running back to pick up five yards on a simple Iso play. Central finally punched the ball into the end zone on a quarterback sneak from the one-yard line with forty-five seconds left in the first half.

When Vickroy's offense got back on the field, they took a knee and let the clock run out in the first half. They were down 21–3, but Coach Thomas knew his team was exhausted, and he just needed to get them back in the locker room to regroup and discuss a new game plan. He could tell that his team was physically worn out, but they were mentally tough. It was obvious that there were strategic adjustments that needed to be made, and Coach Thomas knew exactly what he needed to do.

The team ran into the locker room, and Jimmy immediately began to give everyone encouragement.

"We're still in this game, fellas. Keep your heads up and keep fighting."

Moments later, Coach Thomas came in to the locker room.

"Hydrate. Everyone get those electrolytes in your system. We're gonna need everything we got in the second half. Get with your position coaches for ten minutes. I'll go over game plan adjustments afterward."

The players all broke up into their respective position groups, and the coaches went over position-specific adjustments while the players continued to hydrate and adjust their equipment. After about ten minutes, Coach Thomas came back into the locker room to address the team.

"All right, everybody, bring it in. Listen up. They're running zero blitz on every play. We tried to counter it with screens in the first half, but we couldn't get it going consistently, so let's do it like this. They think their defensive backs can cover our receivers in man coverage all day, but I beg to differ. We'll run the quick game passing attack with underneath routes all day and get the ball to our playmakers and see if they can keep up. Sean, we know the blitz is coming, just get the ball out of your hands in rhythm and let your receivers do the work after the catch. Don't take any sacks, we can't afford to get behind in down and distance. Drags, slants, speed outs, and hitch routes until they come out of that zero coverage.

"Jimmy, EJ, Rogers, Davis, y'all should feel disrespected that they think they can run cover zero all game. Make 'em pay. Defensively we're gonna start sending some pressure of our own. The quarterback is soft, and he is not mobile. If we send pressure and don't give him time, he won't stay strong in the pocket and deliver the football accurately. Jimmy, we're gonna bring you down in the box for run support. Just make sure you're reading your keys and don't get sucked in on play action pass. This is it, men. We been here before, and we've responded every time. Backs against the wall, nothing to lose. We took their best shot, and we're still standing. Shake it off and get ready to punch them back in their mouths for the next twenty-four minutes. Let's go out there and get a stop, get the ball, and drive down and score. Everybody look me in my eyes. Play with fire, discipline! Fire, discipline! Fire, discipline! Let's go! Let's *go*!"

Vickroy ran out of the locker room and back out on the field with renewed energy. When they got to the sideline, Coach Thomas pulled Jimmy to side.

"This is your half. They can't cover you in zero coverage. Put this team on your back and lead us to a championship. You're the best player in the state. It's time to remind everyone. Dominate."

"Yes, sir," Jimmy said as he nodded his head in agreement.

With Central receiving the ball to start the second half, it was critical that the Vickroy defense got a stop to avoid a four-score deficit. On the kickoff, the Vickroy kicker was able to kick the ball through the back of the end zone for a touchback, therefore avoiding the potential for a big return. On the first play of the second half, Central came to the line of scrimmage in a double tight end, single back formation with Austin Lott lined up in the backfield. As the Central quarterback began going through his cadence, Matt Simpson and the other linebackers began to creep up toward the line of scrimmage, preparing to blitz. Central snapped the ball, faked a handoff to the running back, and took a deep shot to the tight end in the middle of the field, but Jimmy read the play perfectly. He was all over the receiver and intercepted the pass after tipping it up to himself before securing the catch. He returned the ball to the Central thirty-five-yard line before being forced out of bounds. The Vickroy sideline went crazy as they got the turnover that they desperately needed and started the second half out with a huge momentum swing.

The Vickroy offense ran out on the field and huddled up.

"All right, fellas, this is our half. Let's shake and bake. Let's go gun spread 938 X drag, halfback check on two, two. Ready."

"Break."

Vickroy came to the line of scrimmage, and just as they did in the first half, Central had all of their linebackers up close to the line of scrimmage, ready to blitz. The corners on the outside were in press coverage, but the safeties were playing the inside receivers in off coverage. Sean knew that with that much space, Jimmy would be able to get open underneath if there was no inside help. At the snap of the ball, Sean saw the middle linebacker shoot right up the middle through the A-gap. Sean caught the snap and hit Jimmy on a drag route, which he was able to take up the field for an easy twelve-yard gain before the safety was able to bring him down. Vickroy hurried to the line and threw it to Jimmy again on the same route, and he picked up another first down inside the Central ten-yard line.

On the next play, Vickroy came to the line of scrimmage in a shotgun trips formation, with Jimmy lined up as the inside receiver. The Central safety that was responsible for covering Jimmy was now playing him much closer to try to take away the quick pass. At the snap, Jimmy broke to the inside, just like he had done on the two previous plays, and as soon as the Central defender looked at the quarterback to play the pass, Jimmy changed direction and went up the center of the field. He was wide open, and Sean threw a dart that hit him right on the numbers for a touchdown. The Vickroy offense had found an answer to the aggressive defensive style of Central Catholic. Now they knew they could move the ball and make it a competitive game in the second half.

When Central got back on offense, the Vickroy defense gave them fits. They sent pressure from a different defender every play, which made it hard for the Central quarterback to read the coverage. A questionable roughing-the-passer penalty helped Central get a first down on a play that would have led to a fourth and long punt situation. After Central running back Austin Lott followed up the personal foul penalty with a strong run, where he bounced off two tackles near the line of scrimmage on his way to a fourteen-yard gain, they were in field goal range. Once they were in field goal range, Central decided to play conservative and run the ball on three consecutive downs. They wanted to avoid the potential of being knocked out of field goal range with a sack. They weren't able to pick up another first down, so on fourth and three from the Vickroy twenty-five-yard line, Central was able to hit a field goal to make the score 24–10.

The Vickroy offense returned to the field and picked up where they left off. Sean connected with EJ on back-to-back hitch routes for a first down. On the next play, Sean hit Davis on a speed out in which he was able to turn into a twenty-yard gain. When Vickroy got to midfield, they came to the line of scrimmage in a shotgun formation, with Jimmy lined up as the inside receiver. Sean started his cadence and then signaled for Jimmy to come in motion. As Jimmy came across the formation, the center snapped the ball, Sean caught it, and pitched it to Jimmy on an end-around. Jimmy caught the pitch and immediately avoided a tackle by the outside linebacker coming off the edge.

From there it was a foot race, and nobody on Central had the speed to catch Jimmy from behind. It was clear that Jimmy was just as fast as he was before as he stuck his foot in the ground and exploded up the hash. He easily outran the Central defenders on his way to the end zone to bring the Patriots within a touchdown. The tension on the Central Catholic sideline was evident. Their once tightly secured lead was starting to slip away, and all of the momentum and confidence was on Vickroy's side.

When Central got back on offense, they came out firing, hitting receivers Allen and Johnson for fifteen and twenty yard gains on back-to-back plays. With a one-possession 24–17 lead, they were starting to feel the pressure and responding with aggression on offense. Central was known to be arrogant, but they were also known to back it up. They weren't going to just let Vickroy come back without a fight. After the two first downs through the air, running back Austin Lott got in on the action with a pair of big runs of his own in which he showed his combination of power and agility by shaking and running over Vickroy defenders. Central was inside of the Vickroy twenty-five-yard line, threatening to put a score on the board and add to their seven-point lead. Already in field goal range, Central continued to play aggressive and took a couple shots to the end zone, but solid coverage by the Vickroy defensive backs forced incompletions.

Facing a third and ten, Central came to the line of scrimmage in a single back formation with a tight end lined up to the left and a slot receiver on the right. On the snap of the ball, the quarterback faked a handoff to the running back and rolled out to his right on a bootleg. As he looked to throw to his tight end on the crossing route, Jimmy and a host of Vickroy defenders brought him down for a sack and five-yard loss. The sack made a field goal try for Central much more difficult, so on fourth down, they kept their offense out on the field, believing that they had a better job of converting on fourth and long than making a thirty-eight-yard field goal. Central came to the line of scrimmage in a double tight end single back formation for the fourth down attempt.

Jimmy knew from his film study that Central liked to run outside zone run plays and play action pass plays out of this formation. Understanding that Central needed fifteen yards for a first down, Jimmy was anticipating play action pass. On the snap of the ball, the quarterback handed the ball off to running back Austin Lott. Lott took the handoff and approached the line of scrimmage before suddenly stopping and pitching it back to the quarterback on a flea flicker. Jimmy read the play all the way. He knew they weren't going to run the ball in that situation, and when he saw the tight end release down the field, he knew the flea flicker was coming. Although Jimmy had great coverage, the quarterback threw it up to give the big tight end a shot to make a play. The 6'5" tight end was much bigger than Jimmy, but what Jimmy lacked in size, he made up for with incredible athleticism. As the ball came down, Jimmy jumped up over the tight end, caught the ball one-handed in the corner of the end zone, and got both feet down before stepping out of bounds. Vickroy would have taken over possession of the football if Jimmy would have just batted the ball down, but the interception was a statement play that proved to everyone watching that Jimmy was back to where he left off before the accident.

Vickroy started the next drive in rhythm, connecting on passes to Davis, EJ, and Rogers as they marched down the field into Central territory with the third quarter winding down. On the last play of the quarter, Sean completed a well-contested pass to EJ on a skinny post to give Vickroy a first and ten at the Central twenty-five-yard line.

As the fourth quarter began with Vickroy on yet another dominating drive, it was clear that they were now in control of the game. Central dominated in the first half, but the third quarter belonged to Vickroy. They scored on every drive, and Central did not seem to have an answer for Jimmy. Defensively Vickroy was able to keep them off balance with a variety of blitz packages. It was clear that the fourth quarter would be decided by which team made the big play in the most critical moment. Luckily for Vickroy, they had the best player on the field.

On the first play of the fourth quarter, Sean looked to get the ball to Rogers on a drag route across the middle, but it was broken up by the Central middle linebacker who faked the blitz but sunk underneath the route after the snap. On the next play, Vickroy ran a double drag route combination, but Central dropped seven into zone coverage, and there was nowhere for Sean to throw the ball, so he threw it away out of bounds. Vickroy had finally forced Central to stop running that aggressive cover zero blitz that they had been running all game, but now it was up to Sean to make the proper reads to find open receivers and not throw into coverage. On third down, Vickroy ran a draw play and were able to pick up eight yards but were short of a first down and settled for a field goal on fourth down. The score was now 20–24 with eleven minutes left in the game.

In the previous year, this matchup came down to the last play of the game, and it looked like the fans at Hershey stadium were in for another thrilling finish in this game.

When Central got back on offense, they tried to get the running game going with Austin Lott, but Matt Simpson was playing like his hair was on fire. Shedding blocker, shooting gaps, and making devastating hits on every play. Vickroy quickly forced a three and out but couldn't get anything going on offense on their next possession either. After scoring a combined forty-one points in the first three quarters, it seemed like both teams had the other figured out, making points a lot harder to come by in the fourth quarter. With four minutes left in the game, Vickroy was able to get on the board with another field goal after Jimmy got them into field goal range by turning a catch on a short dig route into a sixty-yard gain, thus making it a one-point game at 23–24.

The pressure on the Central sideline was undeniable. So far they had been shut out in the second half and squandered an eighteen-point lead. They hadn't lost a game in two years, and they were the clear-cut favorites coming in to the game, but they seemed to be letting the game slip away. Vickroy was still one point behind, so running time off the clock on the next possession was imperative for the Central offense. Vickroy needed to be aggressive enough to stop the run, but they also need to be cautious because giving up a touchdown at this point in the game would most likely wipe out any chance they had at getting a victory.

On Central's first play, they were able to gain eight yards on a play action pass that they completed to their receiver, Allen, on a comeback. After showing their willingness to pass, Central handed the ball off to the running back, Austin Lott, on the next four plays in which he was able to pick up two first downs. The Vickroy defense could not afford to let Central pound the ball all the way down the field and run the clock out, so Coach Thomas called a time-out to talk to the defense.

"Look, it's now or never. They don't wanna pass, but we're gonna have to force them to. We can't let them run the ball and chew the clock. So we're sending pressure from here on out. DBs, *lock it down*! Don't be peaking in the backfield because we know they're gonna go back to play action. Matt, be aware of the screen pass. Jimmy, if they max protect, drop deep and help in coverage. We need a stop right now. No more first downs. If we get the ball back with enough time, we'll go down and score and get this win. All right?"

"Yes, Coach," the defense responded.

"Let's run Pates Mike Sam zero. Matt, make the check if necessary."

"Yes, sir"

The Vickroy defense ran back out on the field with a sense of urgency. Central came to the line of scrimmage in an *I* formation and ran a power run play straight into the Vickroy blitz. Nevertheless, they were still able to pick up four yards on the play. Central was now at midfield with under three minutes left in the game. If they could at least get a field goal, Vickroy would need to drive down the entire length of the field and score a touchdown to win. Central continued to the run the ball and picked up another first down which put them in Vickroy territory. The Central offensive line was so physical that they were able to drive the Vickroy defensive line off the ball, even when facing a blitz.

On the next play, Central came to the line of scrimmage in a strong I formation with the tight end and lead blocker lined up to the right. On the snap of the ball, the quarterback handed the ball to the running back on a misdirection run, the entire Vickroy defense crashed down to defend the run, going to the right as Austin Lott took the handoff and went left. Jimmy came downhill from his safety position and was the last defender in between Lott and the end zone. Open field tackles are extremely difficult to make, especially on someone as shifty and agile as Lott. Jimmy took the perfect pursuit angle and squared up to make the tackle, but instead of securing the tackle, Jimmy punched down on the ball as hard as he could and jarred it loose from Lott's grasp. The ball was loose on the turf for what seemed like forever. The entire stadium went silent as Jimmy and Lott scrambled to get up and recover it. But just before Lott could get to it, Matt Simpson slid in to recover and secure the fumble. Jimmy made the play of the game when they needed it most and gave Vickroy an opportunity to go down and score to win the game.

With just under two minutes remaining in the game, Vickroy started the drive on their own thirty-yard line with two time-outs. They came to the line of scrimmage in a shotgun empty formation. Sean could tell, based on alignment, that the defense was no longer running man coverage. On the snap, Sean caught the ball, stepped up in the pocket, and delivered a strike to Jimmy on a dig route for a ten-yard gain. Vickroy hurried to the line of scrimmage to preserve their time-outs and quickly snapped the ball. Sean attempted to connect with EJ on an out route, but it was well defended and landed incomplete.

On the next play, Vickroy ran the defense off with all vertical routes, and Sean took off up the middle of the field for a twelve-yard gain and another first down. Vickroy then used its second time-out of the half with 1:20 left in the game. On the next play, Sean scrambled for another first down, but this time he was able to get out of bounds and stop the clock. Vickroy had the Central defense reeling. They were gassed and knew that their only hope was that Vickroy would run out of time. On the next play, Vickroy lined up in an empty formation again, but this time, Sean threw the ball to Jimmy on a curl route for an eight-yard gain. Vickroy hurried to the line of scrimmage and spiked the ball to stop the clock. Vickroy was now facing a third and two with under a minute left in the game. Sean was having success running the ball on the drive, so Coach Thomas called a QB draw, but the Central defensive line was able to shed their blocks and tackled Sean in the backfield for a one-yard loss. Vickroy was forced to use their last time-out to stop the clock and come up with a fourth and three play call with the entire season on the line. Coach Thomas called the offense over to the sideline and got in the huddle with them.

"All right, look, I was told a long time ago by another coach that when the game is on the line, to think about calling great players, not great plays. So we're gonna run waggle. Sean, you'll have the option to run it or pass it. If you can run for the first down and get out of bounds, take it. If you can't run it, look for Jimmy or EJ on the crossing pattern. Get the reach block so Sean can roll to the edge. Season is on the line, men. Go get it."

The Vickroy offense ran back out on to the field and came to the line of scrimmage in an I formation. On the snap, Sean faked the handoff to the running back and rolled out of the pocket to his right, he had no intention to pass the ball as he immediately tucked it and started sprinting toward the sideline. Sean pointed to the defender in pursuit, signaling to his receivers to abort their routes and to start blocking. Jimmy made a great block on the defender and gave Sean room to get around the edge and up the sideline. Sean picked up the first down, but he was looking for more. He cut back inside, making another defender miss before being tripped up at the Central twenty-two-yard line.

The crowd was going wild after the amazing play by Sean, but there was no time for Vickroy to celebrate. They had to hurry to the line of scrimmage and spike the ball to stop the clock. They were now in field goal range, but there was still thirty seconds left on the clock. Coach Thomas didn't want to put the game in the hands of the kicker and wanted to take a few shots at the end zone before settling for a field goal attempt. On the next play, Sean completed a pass to Jimmy on an out route in which he was able to get out of bounds to stop the clock after a ten-yard gain. On the play after, Sean rolled out to his right, looked to hit the tight end on a crossing pattern, but the tight coverage forced him to tuck the ball and run it. Sean broke a tackle, got up field for a nine-yard gain, but was unable to reach the end zone or get out of bounds to stop the clock. After the gain, Vickroy hurried to the line and spiked the ball to stop the clock. Vickroy was now down to the Central Catholic three-yard line with four seconds remaining in the game.

Down by one, Coach Thomas sent the field goal team out to attempt the game-winning field goal. From the three-yard line, the kick was nothing more than an extra point, which the Vickroy kicker hadn't missed all season. The kicker lined up, got set, and signaled to the holder that he was ready, but just before the snap, Central Catholic called a time-out. Coaches typically call time-outs just before big field goal attempts because they believe that calling the time-out helps put more pressure on the kicker and increases the chances of a missed attempt. After the brief time-out, again the Vickroy kicker lined up, got set, took a deep breath, and signaled to the holder that he was ready. The long snapper snapped the ball, the hold was good, the kicker made solid contact with the football and pushed it wide right by just a few inches. As the kick sailed just outside of the right upright, the Central sideline stormed the field in excitement. They dodged a bullet and won back-to-back state titles over two great Vickroy teams.

The players on the Vickroy sideline could not believe what just happened. After making so many big plays to come back, they fell three yards short of a game-winning touchdown and inches short of making a game-winning field goal. Jimmy, who finished the game with two touchdowns, two interceptions, a forced fumble, and over two hundred all-purpose yards, congratulated the Central players on their victory and consoled his teammates as they left the field shocked and dejected.

CHAPTER 12

Symphony

After the loss, there was a variety of emotions on the Vickroy side. Some were angry, some were upset, and some were just still in shock. Some of the seniors cried, but it wasn't just because they had lost, they were also emotional because for some of them, this would be their last time ever playing football again. Jimmy wasn't angry like he was in the previous year, but surely he was disappointed. His competitive fire hadn't died in that car crash a year ago, but instead a spirit of peace was born. He wasn't discouraged, he was grateful that God had blessed him and allowed him to make a full recovery from an injury that doctors feared would potentially end his football career. With his football future in jeopardy just months ago, he was happy to have the opportunity to play in the state championship game one last time with his best friends. Although the outcome was not the one that any of them wanted, they knew they had nothing to be ashamed of. Throughout the entire season, they consistently overcame adversity and never stopped fighting and never gave up hope. Coach Thomas and all of New Crofton was proud of them despite the loss.

The mood on the bus ride home was mellow, but unlike last season, the guys talked to one another, and there weren't many tears. The seniors were ending their high school careers without that state title that they all desired but just getting to the big game in back-to-back seasons was no small feat and something they were all proud of. Meanwhile the underclassmen all proved that they had the young talent to make another run at a title next year, and although they had just suffered a loss in the biggest game of their young football lives, they were excited about getting another shot at it next season.

When Vickroy arrived back in New Crofton, there were people lined up along the streets outside of their homes with signs in support of the team as the bus drove by. The players were surprised to see the support from everyone in the town after the loss, but they were grateful to see that everyone was behind them no matter what. As the bus made its way back to the high school, all of the players crowded the windows and waved at everyone who was outside along the route. When the bus pulled in at Vickroy High, they were greeted by cheers of parents and students who filled the entire parking lot. It was an incredible sight.

Before the team got off the bus, Coach Thomas stood up and talked to the guys.

"Men, before we get off of this bus, I want to tell you that I'm proud of you guys. Make no mistake about it, I fully expected us to win the game, and I'm disappointed that we came up short of our goal. But that's life. No matter how hard you work, you'll win some, and you'll lose some. But what's most important is that you guys fought. How you respond in these situations is what defines you as a man. I'm proud that you guys fought all season, fought in this game, and although we lost, you did it with class. I fully expect everyone to take this loss and become better men and better football players because of it. This whole town is proud of you, and although we lost the game, we are still blessed to have the love and support of everyone in this parking lot. Don't beat yourselves up over the loss, enjoy your loved ones, and we'll all get back to work on our next goals on Monday. I love y'all."

The team all unloaded the bus and greeted their friends and family with hugs. Deborah and Emily were there waiting for Jimmy, ready to congratulate him on an inspiring journey that displayed heart and resilience. When Jimmy got off the bus, Emily ran over to give him a big hug and a kiss.

"You played great, how are you feeling?" Emily asked as they walked to the car where Deborah waited.

"I'm okay."

"Good. Your mom said you took it pretty hard last year."

"Yeah. I guess I'm growing."

When Jimmy got to the car, he gave his mom, Deborah, a hug and kiss.

"I know you guys came up short again, but everyone is so proud of you guys, Jim," Deborah said.

"I know, Ma. We gave it our all. I'm disappointed that we lost, but that was my last high school game, and I'm not gonna beat myself up about it. It was a great game, and I had fun."

"Well, I'm glad to hear that."

Jimmy went home with his mom, and they had a good weekend together. They went out to dinner, they went and saw a movie, and they spent all day at church on Sunday together. He didn't think much about the loss; he was more focused on spending time with his mom because he realized that these would be the things he will miss when he's away for college.

When the guys got to school the following week, during the morning announcements, the principal gave a message congratulating the guys on a job well done and a great season. The guys had earned the respect of not only their opponents but of everyone in the town. No one expected Vickroy to have the kind of season that they had, and they proved all of their doubters wrong. All of their classmates congratulated them as they walked the halls, as if they actually won the game. The season that ended in another disappointing finish only added to the admiration of the players and grew the popularity of the program around the area.

Throughout the week, many of the players started to receive scholarship offers from colleges all over the country. With national signing day coming up shortly after the end of the season, colleges liked to get all of their offers out as soon as possible to give student athletes enough time to make the biggest decision of their young lives. Linebacker Matt Simpson received offers to play at Penn State, Rutgers, Michigan State, Syracuse, Boston College, and UConn. EJ received offers from Temple, Buffalo, Miami of Ohio, Bowling Green, Cincinnati, and Wake Forest. Sean's offers included Duquesne, Bucknell, Lehigh, Colgate, Marshall, Rice, and UAB.

Although everyone was excited about the offers they received, they were also anxious to see if Jimmy would regain any of the offers that he lost due to his injury. So far there hadn't been any indication that colleges were as interested as they were last year. Jimmy hoped that he would get the opportunity to play college ball on a full athletic scholarship, but he planned to walk on and play somewhere, even if he didn't get a scholarship. He believed that he had done enough to prove that he was worthy of a scholarship and expected to get a call from someone. It didn't have to be a top school in the country, he was just grateful to be playing again and would have been excited to get a shot anywhere.

On that Friday, Jimmy and Sean met in the hallway to walk to piano class together, which was their final period of the day before the weekend.

"What's up, bro?" Jimmy asked.

"Nothin', man, are you starting track practice next week?"

"Yeah, I told Coach Herman that I needed a week to recover, and he was cool with it."

"Oh, okay, I think I'm gonna run with you this year, bro."

"Oh yeah?"

"Yeah, most of the teams that offered me said they were looking at me at receiver, so I know speed is going to be vital next year. That's gonna be my focus this off season."

"You didn't tell them you're going to be the next Lamar Jackson?" Jimmy joked.

"I know, bro, they're sleeping on me," Sean said, laughing.

"But yeah, I think that's a good idea! Speed will be crucial, no matter what. This is gonna be a fun season!"

"Have you heard anything yet? You better not be holding out on me."

"No, man, not yet. You would be one of the first to know." Jimmy laughed.

"Okay, cool. Maybe the big schools are just waiting to see who they get to sign during the early signing period. You'll probably get all of the big offers in January before national signing day in February."

"Well, I know I didn't have a good-enough season to deserve a scholarship offer from a big-time program, coming off of a career-threatening injury, but we'll see. I'm not stressing over it. I'm on God's plan now."

"Okay, Drake." Sean laughed.

"I'm serious, man, I know no matter what, it's all gonna work out in the best way. Whether it's an offer from a big school, a small Division 2 school, or no offer at all. In the big picture, it's gonna be what's best for me. Gotta have faith, bro."

"You're absolutely right. Stay positive."

Jimmy and Sean got to piano class, sat next to each other, and continued talking.

"Okay, class, put your headphones on and begin warm-ups. We're going to learn a new song today," the piano teacher said.

Jimmy and Sean didn't have much musical talent, but they both signed up for piano class as their elective for the semester because they knew it would be fun, even if they weren't any good at it. As the class began practicing the new song for the day, the classroom phone rang. The teacher answered the phone, said a few words, and hung up. She then walked over to Jimmy and tapped him on the shoulder.

"Yes, ma'am," Jimmy said as he took off his headphones.

"You're being summoned to Coach Thomas's office."

"Oh okay. I'll be right back," he whispered as he nudged Sean and got up from his chair.

When he walked into Coach Thomas's office, he saw Coach Thomas sitting at his desk, talking to another man.

"Hey, Coach, you wanted to see me?" Jimmy asked.

"How are you doing, Jimmy? I'm Coach Cole, defensive backs' coach from the University of Alabama," the man said as he stood up and reached out his hand to give Jimmy a handshake.

"Nice to meet you, Coach," Jimmy said as he gave Coach Cole a handshake.

"The pleasure is mine. Have a seat. How's the leg?" Coach Cole asked as they both sat.

"The leg is great. I would say I'm about 95 percent at this point. I expect to surpass where I was in speed and strength before the accident by the spring."

"Good man, I'm glad to hear that. How many offers did you have last year before the accident?"

"I had about twenty, sir, but all of them withdrew their offers because there was so much uncertainty with my injury."

"And have you heard from any of them since your return?"

"No, nothing official. But I don't know if I would feel comfortable committing to any of those schools after they withdrew their offers when I was at my lowest point. I felt kind of betrayed, you know?"

"I totally understand. Well, let me cut to the chase. Our head coach told me to get on a flight and get here as soon as possible to offer you a full athletic scholarship to play football at the University of Alabama."

Jimmy paused for a moment in disbelief. "Thank you so much, sir," Jimmy said as he bit his lip in an attempt to hold back his emotions.

"The ultimate measure of a man is not where he stands in moments of comfort and convenience but where he stands at times of challenge and controversy. We recruit a lot of great athletes, but our program is built on character. When we play other top 25 teams, they're gonna have great athletes on their sideline as well. We need guys that are more than special athletes. Overcoming what you went through was remarkable, and we want young men like you on our team to help lead us to a national championship. Now we know that once the word gets out that we've offered you a scholarship, a lot more offers will start pouring in. We want to get you down for a visit as soon as possible, if you'd like. We got an offensive and defensive coordinator fighting over you, so I'd like to you to meet both of them as well as the head coach."

"Most definitely. I would love to come down for a visit."

"Okay, sounds good. As soon as I get back, I'll give you a call to set a date. It was nice meeting you, Jimmy. Here is my card. Give me a call or e-mail me if you have any questions or concerns. I'll be your point of contact as we go through the recruiting process. I'll talk to you soon, get back to class," Coach Cole said with a smile as he shook Jimmy's hand.

"Congratulations, Jimmy. You deserve it, kid," Coach Thomas said as he gave Jimmy a hug.

"Thank you so much, Coach Thomas, and thanks again, Coach Cole. This means so much to me," Jimmy said as he left the room.

As Jimmy walked backed to class, filled with excitement, he called his mom.

"Hey, Jim, is everything okay?" Deborah asked.

"Ma, guess what!"

"What?"

"I just got offered a full ride to play at Bama!"

"*Wow*, Jimmy. To God be the glory for the great things He has done! I'm so happy for you, and I'm so proud of you."

"Ma, I can't believe it. Praise God. I didn't think I played well enough to earn a scholarship from a school like Alabama!"

"That's the grace of God. I told you that if we just trust in Him, He'd be there to bless us with much more than we deserve."

"You were right, Ma. I'm so thankful for this journey. I'll let you get back to work. I'll see you at home."

"I love you, Jimmy. Your dad would be so proud. I know he's in heaven, grinning from ear to ear right now. I'll see you when I get home. We'll go out to dinner to celebrate."

"Thanks, Ma. I love you too," Jimmy said with tears rolling down his face.

Jimmy hung up the phone, wiped his eyes, and sent Sean and Emily an urgent text, telling them to meet him in the hallway by the school fountain at the end of the period. When they got out of class, they both went directly to the fountain to make sure everything was okay. When they got there, Jimmy was so excited that he couldn't hold back his smile.

"What's up, man?" Sean asked.

"Is everything okay?" Emily asked.

"Yeah, my bad, did y'all think something was wrong?"

"Well, yeah, your text was kind of dramatic," Emily said.

"I'm sorry, well, nothing is wrong. Just have some news that I wanted to share with y'all, and I couldn't wait."

"What?" Sean said as they both stood in suspense.

"I just left Coach Thomas's office. A coach from Bama was here. They're offering me a full ride!"

"Wow, that's awesome, Jimmy!" Emily exclaimed as she gave him a big hug.

"My man, I knew it, bro! God is good! Congrats, brother," Sean said as he gave Jimmy a hug.

"Thanks, man. I'm still in shock," Jimmy said, laughing.

"Guess what?" Sean said.

"What?"

"I wasn't going to tell you yet, but I'm committing to UAB. We'll be less than an hour apart, bro," Sean said.

"*Oh*. That's gonna be perfect."

"Oh, that's so cute. You two love birds won't have to break up," Emily said, joking.

"Ha ha ha, real funny," Sean said, laughing.

"I'm kidding. I'm so happy for you both. I knew everything would work out."

"Hey, will you guys say a quick prayer with me?" Jimmy asked.

"Of course," they both said as they all joined hands and bowed their heads.

"Lord, we just want to take this moment to say thank you. Thank you for your faithfulness. Thank you for being a God that is always true to your word. Thank you for pursuing us, even when we're too wrapped up in our own lives to pay you attention. Thank you for opening up doors and blessing us above our expectations. Thank you for teaching us that although we may think we know what's best, our lives are much better off in your hands. Thank you for favor, thank you for mercy, and thank you for your grace. We love you, we give you all of the honor, all of the glory, and all of the praise, in Jesus's name. Amen."

*****

A couple of months later, on national signing day, in front of his teammates, coaching staff, family, and media, Jimmy signed his national letter of intent to play football at the University of Alabama. After all he had been through, his dreams were coming to fruition. With the combination of his hard work, dedication, favor and grace of God, he was getting the opportunity to play college football for one of the best teams in the country. Although it was a tough journey, he was grateful for all that he went through. He knew that it was what was best for him as he took his first steps into manhood. His foundation was no longer in his athleticism or skill on the football field. His faith and relationship with God was now the foundation in which his life was rooted. He knew moving forward that no matter what his future in football was, his life was now in God's hands and that He would always work things out for his good. Jimmy was ready to embark on the next chapter of his life equipped with a new outlook, a new purpose, and a new understanding of what God's gift truly is—His amazing grace.

EPILOGUE

—⁂—

In this story, the lead character, Jimmy Lawson, thought that his talent, work ethic, and preparation would be all he needed to accomplish his dreams, but it wasn't enough. He still came up short. Then God stepped in and stripped away everything that Jimmy put his faith in to get his attention. Once Jimmy was able to surrender his life to God, God began to transform him from the inside out. Jimmy became a better man, and God was able to use that to open doors that would not have been opened if Jimmy didn't learn to trust Him.

I was inspired to write this story after a period in my life where I had worked so hard to accomplish my goals but still ended up falling short. I considered myself to be a man of faith, I believed in God, and tried my best to be obedient to His Word, but I realized that I was actually putting my faith in myself and not in God. I didn't trust Him enough to put my dreams in His hands. I wanted to take control of my life by working hard and being dedicated to my craft.

After that didn't work, I found myself in a place where I had no choice but to trust God and truly put my life in His hands. It was at that point that I saw God's grace manifest itself in my life. He opened doors for me that I had no ability to open for myself and blessed me beyond my expectations. I went from feeling like "I don't deserve to be going through these struggles" to "I don't deserve all of these blessings that God is giving me." That's grace. We can't earn it, we don't deserve it, but when we see it, it's nothing short of amazing.

I also found that faith is not only trusting God to bless us with the desires of our hearts, but another level of faith is trusting in God's plan for our lives over our own. This can be uncomfortable, it's in our nature to want to be in control of our own lives; but when we let go and allow God to truly direct our paths, we open up the door to blessings that exceed our imaginations. I encourage anyone reading this to put God first, make your relationship with him your priority, and give Him a chance to prove His faithfulness. Matthew 6:33 says, "*Seek the Kingdom of God above all else, and live righteously, and He will give you everything you need.*" Stop investing so much energy into trying to control every aspect of your life. Work hard at what you do, but seek Him first, and He will bless you beyond your skills and abilities.

God has blessed all of us with different gifts that He intends for us to use for His purpose, for 1 Peter

4:10 says, "*God has given each of you a gift from his great variety of spiritual gifts. Use them well to serve one another.*" But God's greatest gift was the gift of His Son, Jesus Christ.

If there is anyone reading this book that does not know Jesus Christ as your personal Savior, I encourage you to say this prayer and begin a personal relationship with Him.

> Jesus, I believe that you are the son of the living God, sent by the Father from heaven to show me how to live. I believe that you are the Holy Lamb that paid the price for my sins, and I believe that you overcame death. I open up my heart to you and ask that you come in to my life. Forgive me for my sins and help me to live a life that is pleasing to God. Thank you, Lord. In Jesus's name Amen.

If you prayed that prayer, the Bible says in Romans 8:1, "*There is no condemnation for those who belong to Christ Jesus. And because you belong to him, the power of the life-giving Spirit has freed you from the power of sin that leads to death.*" You are now a child of God, accepted into the kingdom of heaven by way of the Son, Jesus Christ. Amen.

ACKNOWLEDGMENTS

There are so many people and experiences that have contributed to this book. From my coaches, teammates, and friends that inspired many of the characters, to my wife, daughter, family, and loved ones that assisted, supported, and encouraged me throughout my entire life. I am extremely blessed to have you all. Through the ups and downs of life, I am thankful that I am able to experience them all with you. Thank you.

Of course, I have to thank my Lord and Savior, Jesus Christ. My foundation, my hope, my joy, and my peace. Thank you for walking with me through the tough experiences that inspired this book, and thank you for not letting me off the hook of completing this project. I pray that my work honors you and brings more souls into your kingdom. It is all for your glory and your honor. Amen.

Mills Family Illustration by Celeste Garcia (2020)
Todd, Ashley, Blake, Maverick, Bishop, and Todd Jr.

Desire. Attitude. Will. Grind.

Wake up that dawg and go to war with yourself.
The only one that can stop you is you.

www.dawgculture.com.

CPSIA information can be obtained
at www.ICGtesting.com
Printed in the USA
BVHW021215170622
640059BV00026B/925